Maid at Christmas

Bell Renshaw

PRAISE FOR MAID AT CHRISTMAS

"I absolutely loved this story!"

JO RUTH, GOODREADS

"…[H]eartwarming with twists to keep you on the edge-of-your-seat, wondering what will happen next."

J.E., GOODREADS

"…[A] fun, Christmasy read to pick up and enjoy when you are in need of a little holiday magic."

AMANDA, GOODREADS

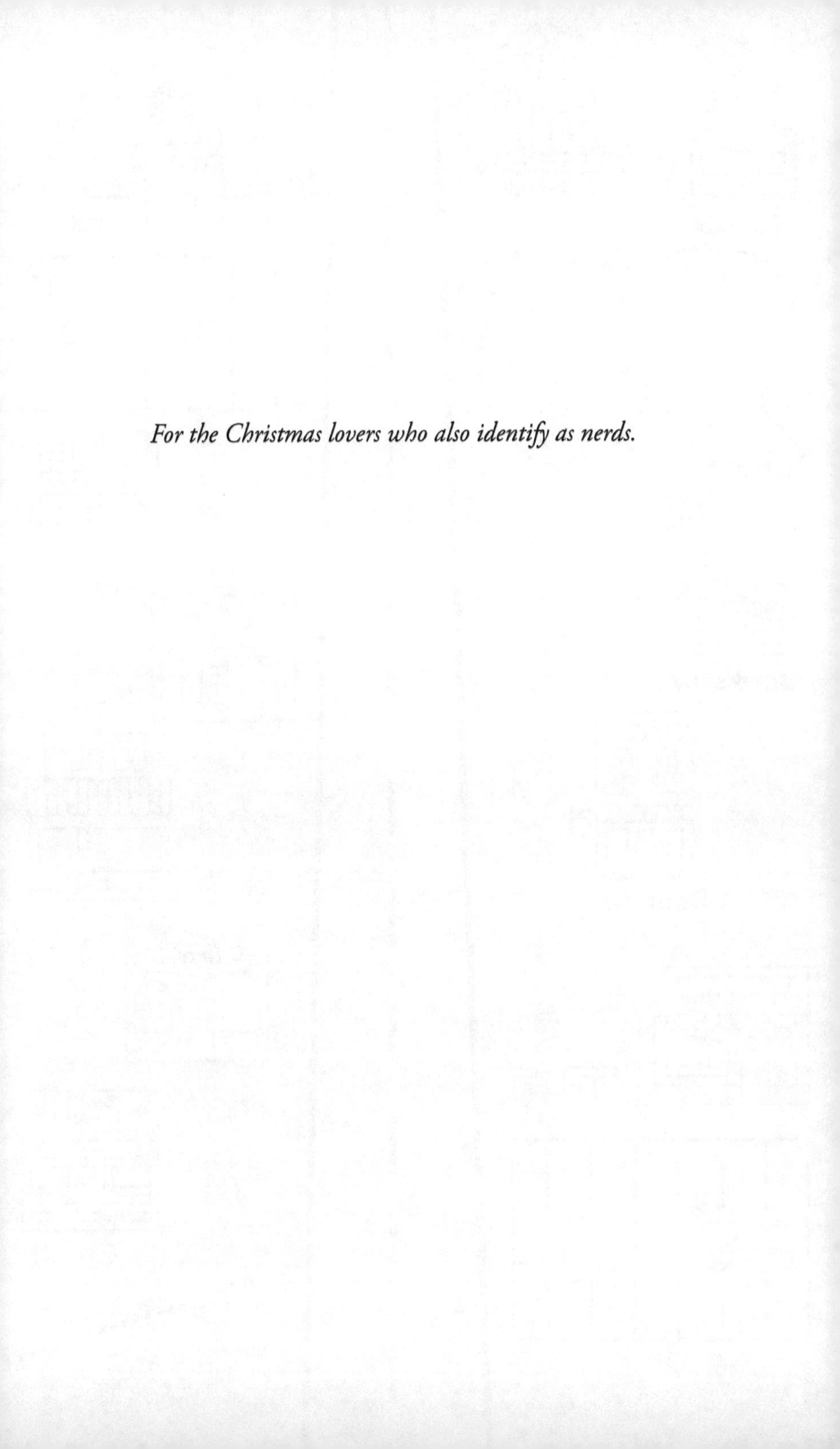

For the Christmas lovers who also identify as nerds.

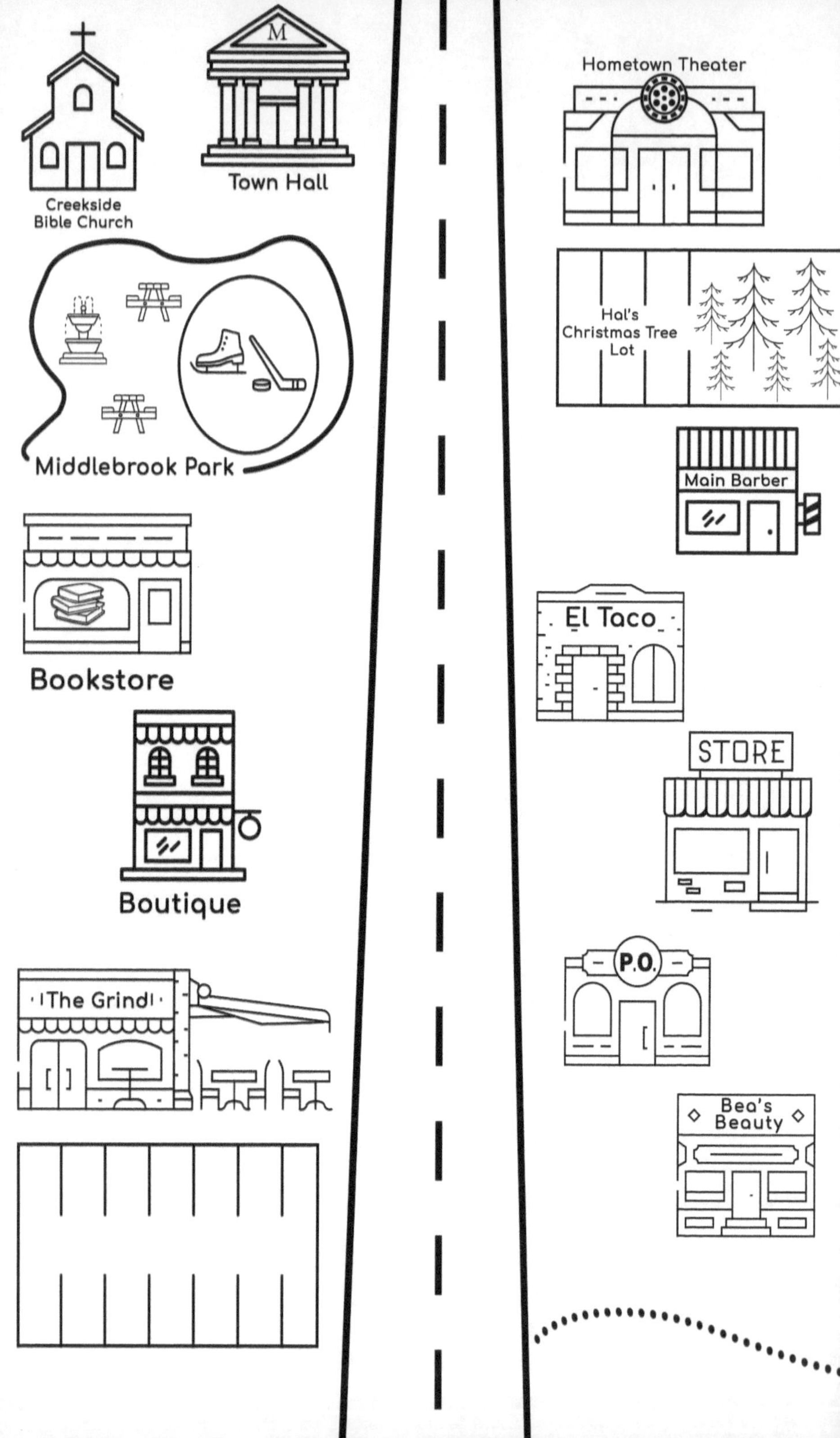

Creekside
Bible Church
Town Hall
Middlebrook Park
Bookstore
Boutique
The Grind
Hometown Theater
Hal's
Christmas Tree
Lot
Main Barber
El Taco
STORE
P.O.
Bea's
Beauty

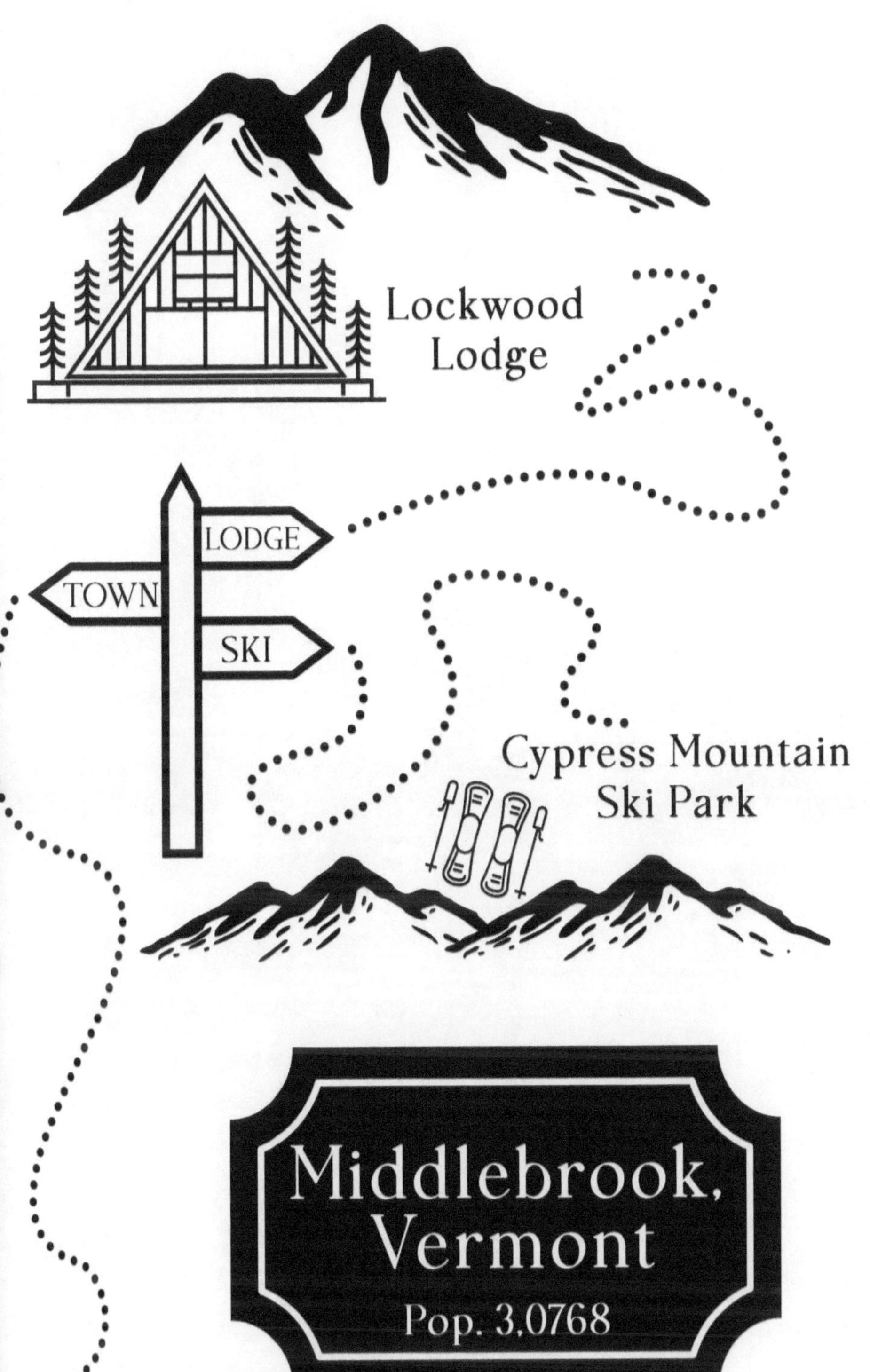

Lockwood Lodge
LODGE
TOWN
SKI
Cypress Mountain Ski Park
Middlebrook, Vermont
Pop. 3,0768

ONE

GOSSAMER LIGHT FILTERED through overhanging branches weighted with snow. Sonora Jackson gripped the wheel of her beat-up, four-door sedan as she wound her way up, up, up into the heart of the snowy Vermont mountains.

"Come on, Wilma, you can make it." She risked moving one hand to affectionately pat the dash of the car in a show of support before another turn demanded her attention.

Bald tires skidded across slick ice, and Sonora let out a yelp. Unperturbed, Nat King Cole crooned *The Christmas Song* through scratchy speakers as Sonora's heart rate slowed with her speed. These roads might just be the death of her.

They'd have to get in line.

She winced. That wasn't the attitude she wanted to carry into her next chapter. Leaving her problems fourteen hundred miles behind was the first step. Tackling a new life without *him* was the next.

But first she needed to actually *make* it to her destination.

A quick glance at her cracked phone screen forced her to do a double take. Risking the motion, she tapped the screen. It was frozen, much like the surrounding landscape. And like she would be if Wilma didn't make it to the lodge. She couldn't remember the last car she'd passed.

Sonora forced her aching muscles to relax as she followed the road. Sheer willpower wouldn't make her car drive any smoother, just as it wouldn't fix the lack of phone service.

Deep breath in. Exhale out.

In. Out.

The tension in her shoulders eased, followed by a smoothing of her wrinkled forehead and—

The car jerked like a giant invisible hand had batted it to the side. Her world slowed even as her vision swam at the force of the spin. Ice. She'd hit a patch of ice, and she had no clue what to do. Screaming at the top of her lungs, she squeezed her eyes shut and braced for impact.

It never came. The car slowed, facing the wrong way, but she was intact.

Have a holly, jolly Christmas…

Sonora slammed a finger to the radio *power* button, and silence flooded the car.

"*Lord in heaven,*" she breathed. Her hand pressed against her breast bone as she refilled her lungs with air. At this rate, she'd never make it to the lodge.

A knock on her car window sent her screaming again, but terror was quickly replaced by confusion. A man in a beanie and puffy black jacket stood next to her car. He wore an expression of bewilderment on his dark features, but his eyes held compassion. Her gaze caught the logo above his heart, and her hopes sputtered to life again.

Making quick work of rolling down the window, Sonora blurted, "You work at the lodge? Can you tell me how to get there?"

The man blinked, a snowflake landing on dark lashes, and then he simply lifted a finger to point across the road. Emotions of relief mingled with embarrassment when Sonora took in the sight. Two massive pillars made of river rock jutted into the sky. Wood beams extended beyond that and were connected by an elaborate metal sign that read *Lockwood Lodge.*

"If you weren't so shook up, I'd have said something sarcastic, but it looks like this little patch of black ice gave you a fright. You all right, darlin'?" The man's voice dipped low, and his breath fogged, but there was true kindness on his soft features.

"I—I think so. I'm from the south—not really sure I know how to drive in this weather." Not to mention Wilma was on her *last* last legs.

"Now *that* I understand. Came up here from Georgia myself. Pretty country, but can't get used to the cold. Anyway, do you need some help gettin' turned around?"

"I think I've got it. Thank you, uh…?"

"Leo."

"Hi, Leo. I'm Sonora."

"Nice to meet ya. You staying at the lodge?"

Sonora appreciated that he tried to keep the doubt from his voice, but she read his skeptical expression like a book as he took in her ratty old college sweatshirt and the dark circles under her makeup-less eyes. She was the furthest thing from the regular clientele at the Lockwood Lodge.

"I'm going to be working at the resort. Housekeeping," she said.

He broke into a wide smile. "Is that so? Well, welcome to Middlebrook, Vermont and The Lockwood Lodge—we'll be happy to have ya."

"Thanks. I'll just…" She motioned toward the road, and he stepped back with a nod.

After a few slow but effective maneuvers, Sonora coaxed Wilma through the massive gate and onto the tree-lined road that led to the resort. It felt like driving through a wintry fairytale forest toward a hidden castle. Everywhere she looked, there was nothing but bare branches and the occasional evergreen, though snow blanketed the forest floor like too much frosting on a gingerbread house. Thankfully, the road remained clear as if it had just been plowed, and soon, she saw the first wooden sign welcoming guests to the lodge.

It was easy to find the sign leading to employee parking, and she sent up a prayer of thanks that Wilma had made it all the way here. It wasn't a trip she was willing to do again anytime soon, but then again, she wasn't planning her next steps. Only her current ones.

She slung her purse over one shoulder and hefted her two small suitcases from the trunk, thankful for the paved and shoveled walkways. Pulling her luggage, she followed the signs with black lettering to the resort entrance.

When she rounded the cover of evergreen trees laden with more snow, her breath caught. The lodge was bigger than she'd expected, with a long walking pathway lined with more evergreens that led to the front doors. Each bushy tree glowed with white lights despite the lingering daylight, and atop each one, a bright red bow acted as a tree topper.

Her attention shifted from the trees to the lodge itself, and she again marveled at its size. It reached three stories high with a covered entrance equally encased in glowing white lights. Twin evergreen wreaths decorated massive floor to ceiling windows on either side of the sliding glass doors, and everywhere, gold and red decorations clung to garland. It swirled up the front posts, arced over the door, and ran along the edge of the covered entrance, wrapping everything in holiday cheer.

She spun to take in the grounds and marveled at the charm. The lodge was massive, yet somehow it held the charm of a small cabin in the woods.

"Sonora!" The shout pulled her back to the entrance.

"Blythe?" Tears pressed against Sonora's eyes as she saw her friend rush toward her through the double glass doors of the resort. Always stylish, Blythe wore skinny navy slacks and a thick cream sweater. Her heeled brown ankle boots clacked with each step, but she didn't seem to care as she rushed forward with open arms.

"I'm so glad you made it all right. Leo called to let me know you'd arrived."

The women embraced, and Sonora wiped her tears when they stepped back. "It's really good to see you."

"You too." Blythe's eyes shone with her own unshed tears, but she flashed her classic, wide smile. "Come on. You're probably freezing, and I can't wait to catch up."

A blanket of warmth greeted the women as they stepped through both sets of double doors—a necessity in the cold Vermont temperatures, according to Blythe. The scent of a pungent fir tree greeted them, along with something that smelled like snickerdoodle cookies.

The lobby was equally as impressive as outside, and Sonora slowed to take it in. The fragrant tree sat decked out in all forms of Christmas ornaments in front of a bank of windows that looked out over a sloping hill leading to a bare deciduous forest. In addition to the large Christmas tree, there were several other smaller ones in nooks around the wide open space.

Groupings of couches took up the rest of the area. They looked inviting and comfortable with extra pillows and blankets artfully draped over the backs of chairs, gathered in baskets, and nestled on couches. A three-story, towering river rock fireplace took up the other side of the lobby pushing out warmth from a roaring fire. Sonora was fairly certain the hearth was at least as tall as her five foot, four inch height, but the size fit the scope of the space well.

"This place is incredible, Blythe. You told me about it, but seeing it for myself is even better."

Blythe beamed. "I'm glad you like it. I've got plans to renovate some areas and would love to update the rooms, but I'm taking it one step at a time."

Sonora turned to look at her friend. The years had been kind to her, softening her once youthful sharpness into soft womanhood. Her red hair was pulled back into an elegant French twist, and her makeup was artfully done, but her smile was the same one Sonora remembered from college—bright and engaging.

"Come on." Blythe extended an arm. "Let's go to my office, and then I can show you to your cabin."

Cabin? Sonora followed her friend behind the front desk counter, but her mind raced. She'd told Blythe she didn't want special treatment, but having her own cabin sounded like the opposite of that. She was about to protest when Blythe broke into her thoughts, half turning.

"Want some coffee? Hot cocoa? We've got a cocoa bar." There was that wide grin again. Blythe's excitement had always been infectious.

"I'm good for now, but thanks." Sonora followed down a corridor lined with dark wood topped by dark green wallpaper. It was masculine yet the gold sconces softened the effect. Blythe stopped at the end of the hall, and with a swipe of a bracelet, Sonora heard the door unlock.

"Have a seat." Blythe motioned to a set of chairs in front of a much smaller fireplace that crackled cozily with yellow and orange flames. "How are you? Gosh, it's been ages since I've seen you. We're not young, naive college girls anymore, huh?"

Sonora winced inwardly at how true her friend's words were. "I think I'm still in shock—this place is amazing."

Blythe laughed. "You sound like me the first time I came up here after Grandpa handed over the keys—metaphorically speaking, that is."

"How did that happen, anyway? I thought your uncle ran this place?" Sonora remembered the stories her friend had told while at college. The beautiful lodge her family owned in Vermont, just minutes from a ski park and quaint small town.

"It's best to say Grandpa *repossessed* it." Blythe shook her head. "It's a long, tedious story, but the lodge *was* run by my uncle for years, and then, last year I think, things were getting dire under his management, so Grandpa took it over again."

"And now you're in charge?" Sonora leaned forward. "I did *not* see that coming."

Blythe laughed, but Sonora caught the edge to it. "I didn't

either, but dear Grandpapa had other ideas. Enough about me. What about you? How are you doing?"

The question Sonora had been dreading. "I'm…okay."

"Come on, Sonnie, you've been my best friend since college. I know we kind of lost touch for a few years there, but one minute you were engaged to Mr. Perfect, getting ready for the wedding of all weddings in New Orleans, and now you're here in Vermont. What happened?"

The weight of Blythe's compassion crushed Sonora, and she fought back tears borne of humiliation. How had her life gotten to this point?

"I'd like to know the answer to that myself." Sonora made a face so that Blythe would know she was joking, but it was clear her attempt had failed. "Jonah…he wasn't who I thought he was. I called things off six months ago and thought I could make it on my own, but my student debt crippled those plans. I saw that Facebook post you made and followed the link to the website. Saw you were hiring and thought if I had a reason to leave Louisiana, I should do it. And here I am."

Blythe's eyes narrowed. "I feel like there's more you're not telling me."

Sonora leaned back in her chair, turning to stare into the flames to give herself a few moments. There was a world of things she'd left out, but they were the ugly details of her own failure. When she met Blythe's assessing gaze, she saw compassion there as well as concern, and the dam broke.

"Jonah was controlling, B. Like, beyond anything I could have imagined. I thought," her voice cracked, "he really loved me, but our relationship wasn't about us. It was about him and the appearance of success." Sonora choked back a sob.

"I'm so sorry, Sonnie." Blythe reached across the space to squeeze her hand.

She smiled at the nickname. She hadn't been called that in years. "I am too."

"Are you sure that you really want to work here though?"

Blythe's expression was earnest. "You're welcome to stay as long as you need to."

A deeper warmth than the fire could provide flooded through Sonora. Her friend's compassion was exactly what she needed and the reason she *wanted* this job.

"I'm positive. I need to pay down my debt, and I don't expect handouts."

"You know that's not what it would be." Blythe nailed her with a sharp gaze.

"I do." Sonora offered up a smile of her own. "This place is perfect, B. And when I said Jonah was controlling, I mean *really* controlling. It's been months since we broke up, but he was still trying to control my life and get back together. I can't live like that. I needed to get away, but I also expect to work."

"If you're sure?" Blythe assessed her a minute longer then nodded once, as if seeing what she'd expected. "We're pretty isolated here. Middlebrook is fifteen minutes away—it's super cute, and you're going to love it—and Cypress Mountain, the ski park, is about the same distance in the opposite direction. Because of that isolation, we have these." She dangled a rubberized bracelet between them.

"What is it?" Sonora took it and saw the resort's logo on it.

"I call them security bands, but some of the staff call them tracking bracelets." She grimaced. "Their reach spans the resort grounds and some of the surrounding woods. It may seem a little extreme, but it has several functions. Since you'll be on house-keeping duty, it will let you enter any rooms that you're assigned to clean. It will show certain light patterns if we have meetings or someone on staff needs to meet with you, but it will also act as a beacon."

"Beacon?"

Blythe hesitated. "Last year, there was a terrible snowstorm, and one of the staff got stranded in the blizzard trying to go between her cabin and the main lodge. If she'd had a beacon like this, we could have found her sooner. She's all right, but she did suffer some frostbite. Right after that, Grandpa found these bands and put them into use."

"That makes sense then." Sonora eyed the bracelet. It was thin and rubbery with a bulb in the middle.

"I promise we're not spying on you." Blythe laughed, but Sonora couldn't find the humor. Not after what Jonah had done. "The Lockwood is a great place to work, but if at any time you think it's not for you, let me know. I'm here for you, Sonnie. Remember that."

"I know." Sonora grinned up at her friend. "Thanks for the job."

Blythe waved her off and popped to her feet. "Are you ready to go see your cabin? We've got a week to prepare for our next big event, and I'd love to get you acquainted with the grounds and your duties. And the hot cocoa bar—because seriously, that's one of the best perks of the job."

Sonora stood and took hold of her suitcases. "Let's go."

TWO

ONE WEEK LATER

"I'm going to be honest—I can't tell if you're joking or not."

"I'm not joking." Graham Hastings leaned back against the plush leather seat in the mid-sized private jet as he studied the slightly blurry video of his friend and right-hand man, Marcus Oswald.

Marcus ran a hand over his face, his image momentarily jumping, as his other hand, the one no doubt holding his phone, dipped and jerked up again.

"Your timing is…"

"Impeccable?" Graham supplied.

Marcus narrowed his eyes. "That wasn't the word I'd have chosen."

Graham turned to look out the small window. They had landed a few minutes prior, and he'd been informed by the lone flight attendant that they would be arriving at the hangar in ten minutes where his car would be waiting.

He checked his watch before stopping himself. Time didn't matter—not this week.

"I know this is not the news you were expecting, but I've been doing a lot of thinking, and I believe it's the right move." Graham tried to analyze the emotions of his friend's angular features, but Marcus never gave anything away. It's what made him so good at his job.

"I mean, I can't say that I'm *that* surprised."

"Come on." Graham leaned forward in his seat and undid his seatbelt. "You had no idea what my answer was going to be."

"Not true. I had a feeling."

Graham rolled his eyes. "You and your feelings."

"You've been unhappy for the better part of the last three years, Graham. Don't think I didn't notice."

Graham flexed his jaw. "Was it that obvious?"

"Not to anyone else. I have the *privilege*," he said it like it was anything but, "of knowing you outside of work, and I think that's where I've seen the greatest toll. You used to enjoy reading for fun and going to museums in your free time, but VyCorp has taken over, well, everything."

"You can say that again."

"Sir?" The attendant approached but remained at a respectful distance until Graham waved the man forward. "We've arrived. We're transferring your luggage now. If you'd like to wait a few minutes—"

"I'll go now. Thank you."

"Very good."

Graham turned back to Marcus. "My car's here."

"How far is it to the retreat?"

"Someone told me an hour from the airport. When is your flight due to come in?"

"Tomorrow afternoon. I still can't believe you're having me come to this thing." Marcus narrowed his eyes. "I don't think I'm going to fit in."

"Actually, you'll fit in just fine if it's run as they claim."

Graham stood, his back aching from sitting so long. What he wouldn't do for a run. Bending low, he looked out the window again just as a few snowflakes began to fall.

Right. Definitely not running outside in this weather.

"What should I do?" Marcus' tone had changed, and Graham paused at the door to the steps, briefcase in one hand, phone in the other.

"Nothing right now. There are still things to negotiate, but I'd like the sale done before the new year."

"And there's your father to consider."

Graham hissed in a breath. The mention of Lawrence Hastings always acted like a slap to the face. "Let's keep this under wraps for now."

"You sure that's how you want to play this?" Marcus's question was gentle, but it held the confidence of a best friend, not an executive secretary.

Graham took a moment to consider his answer, even though he was starting to shiver in the cold coming in through the open plane door.

Keeping things from Lawrence—*Father*—never ended well, but Graham didn't actually need his father's approval for this decision. Lawrence had seen to that the day he'd dumped his failing tech company on Graham's shoulders, jumping ship like Captain Jack Sparrow.

As CEO of VyCorp, Graham had quickly shifted the focus of the company from physical products to digitally-based ones and had seen VyCorp surge to relevance. Now inching toward competition with the five major tech companies, VyCorp was a dream come true.

The problem was, it wasn't Graham's dream.

"I'm sure. He's got no part in this deal."

"All right." Marcus pursed his lips with a nod. "For what it's worth, I think you're doing the right thing. See you tomorrow."

Graham's gut twisted even as his friend's support eased the tightness in his chest. He *knew* it was the right choice, even if it was the last thing his father would approve of, but Marcus' support solidified things in his mind.

Hastings men never gave up, especially when there was money to be made, but Graham wanted more than fame and success. He wanted relevance. He just wasn't sure where to find that.

Graham slid his phone into his pocket and nodded to the attendant. He smiled, saying, "Please be careful, sir. It's slick."

Graham took his time descending to the tarmac and paused as he reached the pavement. Daylight was already fading, and the stiff wind cut straight through his high-end pea coat. The chill was unlike anything he'd felt in a long time. Living in Los Angeles meant he didn't see cold or snow on this level, but there was something refreshing about the chill. It snapped him to attention and caused him to remember that life was fragile. You had to seize opportunity while there was still time.

He'd wondered over the last year if turning forty-two had somehow broken him. It wasn't even mid-life, God willing, but something about this year had sent Graham's heart into restlessness. Each day at the office left him more exhausted. Every decision was tedious. And, as Marcus had pointed out, his pleasure reading and other interests had suffered.

Selling VyCorp, while beyond risky and foolish, seemed like the only answer. But what was next?

A sleek black Lexus waited several feet away, the driver shifting from one foot to the other as he waited for Graham to approach. The man's discomfort pushed Graham forward and he nodded in greeting. The driver opened the back door for him with a brief nod before rushing back to the driver's seat.

Graham slid into warm luxury and released a foggy breath as heat from the vents combatted the cold. His Rolex was still set to west coast time, and rather than adjusting it, he took the expensive watch off and dropped it into his suitcase. This week wasn't about anything other than relaxing and refocusing.

There were decisions to make—another reason why Marcus would be joining him—but Graham planned to make his friend relax alongside him. They both worked too hard, but that was about to change.

The midsized buildings of the city, each topped with a

generous amount of snow, faded into countryside scenery and Graham let his mind wander. This was the first true vacation he'd taken in years, and he wanted to sink into the moment.

Evergreens heavy with snow lined up alongside bare branches as the road wound deeper into forested areas, leaving the snowy meadows behind. It felt like he was disappearing into a winter wonderland worthy of the song.

Sleigh bells ring, are you listening?

His eyes slid closed.

In the lane, snow is glistening…

His phone buzzed to life in his pocket, causing him to jolt upright. He pulled it out and saw her name on the screen. He barely suppressed a groan as he pressed accept.

"What is it, Monique?"

"Is that any way to answer the phone?" Her syrupy-sweet voice poured through the small speaker and caused instant frustration to tighten his muscles.

"It was the nicest thing I could think to say to you." He ground his teeth and forced himself to take a deep breath in through his nose.

"I miss you."

He could imagine her pout. Eyes wide and sparkling with her makeup expertly done to highlight sharp cheek bones and puffy lips. She used her beauty like anesthetic to numb men to any other reality than life with her. He'd fallen for her faster than he'd like to admit, but their relationship's short timespan had only made the breakup easier.

"I'm sure you do." He pressed his eyes closed for a moment. He needed to be civil. "I thought Marcus made it clear to you—we're done."

"But we don't have to be, baby. I've got a red carpet event next month. Come with me?"

His eyes sought refuge in the tree line zipping past. The depths, darkening as the sun dipped below the horizon, cast eerie shadows, but it still looked more inviting than this conversation.

"Thank you, but no."

"Whatever Marcus told you was a lie. I don't know how you can trust him anyway—he's so *beneath* you."

Graham winced. Her unkind words were not only unfair but also untrue. Still, he found her tactic almost humorous.

"You're going to talk to me about what's beneath me? You want to know what else is beneath me, Monique? How about a girlfriend who charged almost a million dollars to my credit card in one month. One. Month. And you know what else is beneath me? Having that same girlfriend tell her friends—in a public restaurant where my friends and colleagues frequent, mind you—that she's going to trick me into marrying her by the end of the year."

Graham's blood boiled at the memory of Marcus relaying the awkward and painful news to him after he'd accidentally overheard Graham's girlfriend.

"He was lying. I never said—"

"He has no reason to lie. Unlike you. I know everything, Monique." Her silence spoke volumes. "While I won't stoop to being petty and will pay off the debt you incurred while we were together, I don't want to see you again. I hope that's clear enough for you."

"You're losing the best thing that could have happened to you, Graham Hastings. When I land this next role, you're going to see that and regret letting me go."

The call disconnected, and Graham dropped his phone into his pocket. She hadn't apologized. Hadn't tried to make things right between them. He should have known better. The string of ex-boyfriends left in her wake should have been his first clue, but it had felt good to have someone so beautiful choose him out of a crowd at a party.

Then again, maybe that had all been fabricated too. He was never dating an actress again.

Eyes closed, Graham tried and failed to push the image of his ex-girlfriend from his mind. Intellectually, he knew it was foolish to miss the woman who had only been after him for his status and, to a greater degree, his money, and yet his heart still ached.

No. That wasn't right. The emptiness there wasn't from missing Monique, it was something deeper. Loneliness. He was alone at Christmas, *again*, and what did he have to show for it? Money.

The thought of selling VyCorp surged to life again with both anxiety and excitement. It was the change he needed to start seeking a more fulfilling life, but it was the opposite of what he'd been taught growing up.

Hastings men didn't retire—certainly not at forty-two. Hastings men fought tooth and nail to make their next million and the next after that. They ignored personal connection, stepped on the backs of those less fortunate, and scrambled for success at the cost of everything.

But he was going to break that cycle.

"The Lockwood Lodge, Mr. Hastings." The driver glanced back at him through the rearview mirror before turning onto a long, tree-lined drive. It curved up the mountain through a forest of frozen trees that sank deep into a blanket of snow.

White Christmas lights illuminated the trunks of the trees as they rounded a bend, and the Lockwood Lodge appeared through the windshield. It was everything the online brochure had said and, perhaps, even more.

A row of evergreens decorated with red bows led the way toward the front of the resort like landing beacons for Santa's sleigh. His driver slowed and approached the circular turn with caution, stopping so that Graham's door was aligned with the entrance. Two nutcrackers stood at attention to the sides of the entryway, and the red and gold decorations nestled into garland added a touch of elegance while maintaining a cozy Christmas feeling.

"Sir." The driver said, his breath puffing out in the cold after he'd rushed to open Graham's door.

"Thank you." Graham stood and slipped the man a hundred dollar bill for a tip.

The driver's eyes went wide, and he bobbed a quick thank you before rushing to get Graham's bags from the back.

"Shall I take these inside for you?"

"I've got them." Graham took the rolling suitcase and slid the strap of the leather satchel over his shoulder before picking up his briefcase and turning toward the entrance.

"Merry Christmas, Mr. Hastings."

Graham winced at the open use of his last name, but thankfully, no one was around. "The same to you."

A brush of warm air greeted him as Graham entered the lobby smelling of fir and cinnamon. If he was going to start the next part of his life in the new year —whatever that was going to look like —this was the perfect place to end the current one.

He'd start fresh with no cumbersome girlfriend and no more expectations from his father. It was his life to live, and he was going to live it to the fullest…whatever that meant.

THREE

GRAHAM STIFLED a yawn with a hand as he consulted the resort map the woman at the front desk had given him. The room for their first scheduled meeting was supposed to be just around the corner from his suite, but he was fairly certain he'd taken a wrong turn somewhere.

"Graham?"

He looked up from the map and into the smiling face of a beautiful woman. She had dark red hair, light green eyes, and a wide smile outlined with dark red lipstick. He could tell that her shoes were designer—Monique had purchased three pairs on his credit card—but the rest of her outfit represented her management position at the Lockwood.

"Hi. I think I'm lost."

"You're almost there." She laughed easily and held out a hand. "This way."

He fell into step next to her.

"I'm Blythe Lockwood, operations manager here at the Lockwood Lodge."

"I met your grandfather a few years back." He could easily imagine the intimidating older man with a full head of white hair and sharp green eyes.

"Meeting Archie Lockwood is always an experience. Welcome." She stepped aside and he entered the meeting room, thankful they'd come in the back, not the front, and his entrance made little commotion.

Graham was immediately hit with the familiar feeling he always got at events where the wealthy congregated—an instant coiling of his stomach and clenching of his hands. It took him back to countless parties and soirées when his father had used him as a prop at the best of times and a crutch at the worst.

"Please, have a seat, Graham." Blythe's smile radiated warmth as she gestured to an empty chair and then moved past him to the front of the room.

He sat next to an older woman with salt and pepper hair, her hand wrapped around that of a man sitting next to her. On his other side, a young businessman who looked to be in his early thirties pushed up wire-rimmed glasses as his attention shifted to the front of the room with everyone else.

"Welcome to the Lockwood Lodge and the Libertas Retreat, everyone." Blythe's smile was warm, and Graham relaxed back against the comfortable seat. "And this is guest services manager, LaToya."

He turned to see a young black woman at the back of the room as she closed and locked the door he'd come through. She smiled at Blythe with a quick nod of her head.

"We are now safe from prying eyes and nosy ears." Blythe laughed, and most of the crowd did as well. "For those of you who are new to this retreat week, I want to offer a big Vermont welcome. This may be my first year hosting, but LaToya has been at the Lockwood for several years and is an expert. We're committed to seeing this retreat through and don't expect any issues."

Graham crossed one ankle over the other and checked his watch, only to remember he'd stowed it in his briefcase. Internally chastising himself for caring about the time when he literally had no obligations, he refocused on what Blythe was saying.

"Being a Lockwood, I know the power of last names. I also know how hard each and every one of you here desires to have time away from the pressures of those surnames and, to be frank, the wealth that comes with them." Blythe's expression turned serious. "It's why my grandfather created the Libertas Retreat. Libertas —Latin for freedom—is a floating week throughout the year where those who hold the weight of wealth and other burdens may come and set them aside to rest and relax in anonymity."

Blythe crossed to the other side of the room, her manner relaxed but confident. "There is no prestige here. No power dynamic. Just a group of people seeking the same thing—freedom. You're all here by personal invitation, and we operate on a strict policy of confidentiality."

"Yes." LaToya moved to the front of the room. "Only Blythe and I know your true identities and our staff are only given minimal details about this retreat and have signed NDA's. You will only be using first names here—though some have opted to choose a new name for the week—and upon registration you also signed a non-disclosure agreement. If you have questions about that, you can speak with me after."

"The purpose of all of this," Blythe paused to look around the room, "isn't for cloak and dagger theatrics, but to keep you all safeguarded. For the first part of the week, we haven't accepted reservations, though that changes on Wednesday when a few holiday guests will arrive. Still, no one will be privy to your true identity, your net worth, or even where you live. We ask that you, too, take part in this. Don't discuss business with one another in any form or fashion. Don't divulge your true identity to anyone. Treat this as a retreat, not the means to network. If, at the end of the week, you'd like to exchange information, we welcome that, but for the duration of the week, we ask that you enjoy the freedom of obscurity."

"What if it comes up naturally?" A gray-haired man a few rows in front of Graham barked his question.

"We understand that you have all seen financial success. It's tempting, when brought together with others like you, to discuss those things. Please refrain. Natural or not, business is not a discussion topic at the Lockwood." Blythe looked around the room again. "Any more questions?"

"Do we have to do all these activities?" The older woman next to Graham asked, waving a sheet of paper.

"Not at all," LaToya answered with a bright smile. "We've set up excursions and activities, both inside and out, but they are only options. If you'd rather take part in our hot cocoa bar each day and read a book in the lobby, you're welcome to do that instead."

"Oh good. I've got three books I aim to finish." The woman let out a contented sigh, and Graham held in a laugh.

"If there are no further questions, please feel free to mingle here or explore the lodge. Our schedule starts in the morning for those who are interested. And one last word of advice." Blythe clasped her hands in front of her. "I know from personal experience how easy it is to default to business as a discussion topic, especially your own business, but know this: you are more than your businesses, or the company you run, or the inheritance you've received, or the money you've come into. Dive deep into what makes *you* unique and make new friends here without the worries of what happens after. We promise it will be worth it."

"If you need anything at all, any of the Lockwood staff can help you, but if it is specific to this week's retreat, please be sure to seek out Blythe or me," LaToya said.

Graham took in a deep breath. This was going to be an interesting challenge. So much of his life was business, or related to business, but this week was anything but.

"Hello," the woman next to him said. "How did you hear about the weekend?"

Graham gauged the best response to her question, considering what Blythe had just said. "I met Mr. Lockwood several years back. He suggested this week to me, but this was the first year I could take him up on an invite."

"I see." Her eyes narrowed.

Graham immediately wondered if he'd given too much away. "And you?"

"A friend of a friend recommended it." Her calculating look shifted. "I'm here for the quiet. And the reading." She nodded over her shoulder to the man she was sitting with. He'd fallen into conversation with another man who looked to be near Graham's age. "He's here because I make him take a break every two years."

"I hope this week is relaxing. For you both."

"Same to you." The hard planes of her face softened. "Enjoy this time. If you're anything like my husband, you've run yourself ragged and need to recoup. Besides, who knows what you could find while in the snowy Vermont forest."

She smiled, the effect transforming the aloof look she'd worn before, and Graham found himself smiling back.

He liked the sound of that. Who knew what he could find here?

FOUR

SONORA ROLLED her neck from side to side, but the pain wouldn't go away.

"You okay, Sonora?"

"Yeah. Thanks, Kayla." Sonora forced a smile to reassure the young mother. She worked part-time at the resort for a little extra cash and always looked chipper.

"I think we're going to the coffee shop in town if you want to join us? They have a nighttime happy hour where they serve decaf drinks and yummy treats. It's a lot of fun."

Sonora's heart warmed at the invitation. She'd worked at Lockwood a full week now, and while she did want to make new friends, her body was screaming for a night off.

"I think I'm going to curl up with a book tonight, but next time, I'm in."

"I'll hold you to that," Kayla said with a grin. "Night."

Sonora watched as Kayla slung her bag over her shoulder and left the locker room with a wave. She truly seemed to enjoy her job, and Sonora hoped she could get to that level of devotion as well.

Sonora changed into a cozy sweatshirt and thick leggings, slipping her feet into knock-off fur-lined boots before grabbing her tote and heading for the door. But she paused in the hallway. She'd turned down the invite to socialize, but she also didn't want to retreat to her lonely cabin.

While she was thankful that Blythe had given her a small cabin on the premises, complete with a galley kitchen and mini sitting area, she wanted the perfect middle ground that came from being near people but not having to talk to them.

Shifting directions, Sonora headed toward the hot cocoa bar. She'd already had dinner with the rest of the cleaning crew in the staff lounge, but a sweet, chocolate drink sounded like the perfect way to end the night.

Blythe had said she was welcome to use any of the sitting areas and the amenities when she was off duty, likely a perk of knowing the boss, but up until this point, Sonora had kept her distance. It felt awkward being among the guests who could afford a week at the lodge right before Christmas. That changed tonight.

The selection of the cocoa bar exceeded anything Sonora could have imagined. There was the regular hot cocoa base in one airpot, but also a dark cocoa, white cocoa, and peppermint cocoa to choose from. In addition to that, glass jars with lids filled the counter, offering a staggering variety of add-ins and toppings from the typical marshmallows and candy canes to more exotic options like crystallized ginger, orange extract, and coconut.

Selecting a tall glass mug, Sonora opted for peppermint cocoa and topped it with marshmallows. She popped a candy cane in for good measure. The sweet scent took her back to chilly days as a kid when her mother would welcome her home from school with a mug of hot cocoa made from the cheap, powdered mixes. The memory caused a sharp ache in her chest.

She pushed the thoughts away and chose a leather loveseat near the window. The lights were dim, but the lamp next to the chair would make reading easy. Outside, through the floor to ceiling window, Sonora could just make out lightly falling snow. She felt like it hadn't stopped snowing since she got here, but without anywhere to go, she didn't mind. Most of her day was spent inside anyway.

Pulling the worn paperback from her tote, she took a sip of the sweet cocoa and let the book fall open to the scrap of paper she used as a bookmark. Setting it aside next to an errant bottle of syrup, she sank into another reality.

Subconsciously, she knew time passed, but in the world of her novel, Sonora had no concept of time or her surroundings. As a kid, she'd always escaped into books, and even now as an adult, she found it was comforting to find happiness between the pages of a novel. The evils that lurked there were surmountable.

"Could you pass the maple syrup?"

Sonora screamed and threw her book up in the air. Heart pounding, she gripped the arms of her chair and looked up into the face of her attacker. Up and up until she met soft, sun-dipped brown eyes, dark brown hair touched with gold and graying at the sides, and close-cropped facial hair barely hiding a smile. He looked several years older than her but wore the age well.

One handsome attacker.

Reality filtered in through the haze of her fright, and Sonora blushed. She felt the heat creep up her neck to her cheeks and all the way to the roots of her blonde hair. She had just *screamed* at the handsome man.

"I'm so sorry." He placed a hand flat against his chest and took an immediate step back.

She happened to notice it was his left hand and devoid of a ring. *So what?*

"Are you okay? Clearly, you didn't hear me approach." He looked like he was trying to hold back a laugh.

"I get really into reading. I'm so sorry." She dropped her forehead into her hands, willing the crimson shame to fade. "Did you ask me for maple syrup?" She risked a glance up and caught the smile again. It had grown and only made his angular features more attractive. There were faint wrinkle lines at the corners of his eyes, and she guessed he was several years older than her, but there was a youthful quality to his eyes as they poured into hers.

He pointed. "It's just right there, and ironically, I didn't want to scare you by reaching for it."

Sonora remembered seeing the syrup on the table beside her and blushed again. "Right. I'm sorry."

She offered up the glass bottle, determining only to meet his gaze for a moment, but the depths of his eyes drew her to study them. They looked kind and inviting—or was that just what she wanted to see?

"Thanks." He accepted the bottle but hesitated. "What were you reading that had you so engrossed?"

There it was again. An all-consuming blush threatening to flood back in, even though she had no reason to be ashamed of her reading choices. But the title…

"*A Wife for the Knight*. It's…a fantasy romance." She choked the words out and saw the corner of his lip twitch.

If only magical powers would consume her like they had the young maiden in her book. Then she could turn invisible or magic away his memory of this moment.

"It must be good to have your attention like that."

She narrowed her gaze. There was no judgment in his words. "It is. I've read it a few times." She held up the tattered paperback as proof.

"I've got one of those myself." He held up his own book, and she almost laughed. It was a tattered copy of a space opera she'd read more than once.

"I love that series."

"You've read it?"

"A few times." She shrugged and pushed a strand of hair behind her ear, feeling his gaze on her.

"It's the perfect escape."

There was something in his voice that made her look up. He wore a far-off look that she knew well. The same one, she guessed, that was her reason for reading. To step out of the reality of life for even just a short time and live in someone else's skin.

"It is," she agreed.

But what did this handsome man have to escape from? She let her gaze travel over him, more assessing this time. He wore dark wash jeans, leather shoes that looked well-worn, and a thick cable knit sweater in a dark green color that showed off his tan.

He caught her looking, and the slight incline of his head had her fighting back yet another blush. She needed to escape this conversation before it got more awkward.

"Sorry." She stood. "I interrupted your hot cocoa time."

"Not at all." He held out a hand just shy of touching her arm. "You don't have to go."

"I needed a refill anyway." She held up her mug but paused. "But I have to ask—maple syrup?"

He grinned and fell into step next to her as they made their way back to the bar. "I know how to make a mean cup of maple cocoa."

"Oh? I've never heard of that." She looked up, and their eyes met with an electric jolt of *connection.*

Her breath shallowed even as she told herself to get a grip. He stood several inches taller than her, and this close to him, she caught the musky scent of his cologne. He smelled like an expensive forest that she could get lost in.

"Let me prove it to you." He took her cup, eyes never leaving hers, before he set to work. "You've got to start with the dark hot cocoa or else it can be too sweet." He filled their mugs with the rich, brown liquid and then held up the maple syrup. "Then a little maple syrup, butterscotch chips, and a few marshmallows to top it off."

"I have my doubts." She accepted the mug from him and flashed a skeptical look before taking a sip. Sweetness rushed over her tastebuds, but he was right. The maple balanced the bitterness of the dark chocolate, and the butterscotch added just the right touch of flavor. "Wow. This is delicious."

"What can I say? I'm a chocolate connoisseur." His gaze bored into her over his own mug as he took a quick sip.

Marshmallow stuck to his beard, and she giggled. "You've, uh, got something there."

"Hazards of good hot cocoa." He wiped it away with a napkin. "I'm Graham, by the way. Frightener of young women reading." He placed his hand flat against his chest again and offered a slight bow.

She laughed at the dramatics. "I'm Sonora, said reader."

He extended his hand, and she accepted the shake. Warmth rushed up her arm from where their palms met. His hand engulfed hers in a gentle but firm shake. The kind a businessman learned to perfect, or so she guessed, for that's who he had to be. There was an easy confidence about him, and while his clothes didn't advertise designer labels, she could tell they were quality pieces.

When he released her hand, she felt the sting of disappointment but chastised herself for the reaction. He was clearly a guest here—a wealthy one, no doubt—but he didn't come off as snooty.

"Did you want to sit?" He gestured to the chair she'd vacated and the one next to it.

She did, but a yes lodged in the back of her throat. Her ex had been this charming. He'd also had the same amount of confidence Graham exuded. It was all the reminder she needed that her guy-radar was broken, maybe irrevocably so, and it was better to back away now.

"Sonora?"

Her eyes sought the escape she couldn't have planned any better. "Blythe." Her friend's name was a lifeline.

"Sorry to interrupt." Blythe stepped up to them, her gaze shifting from Graham to Sonora and widening only enough that Sonora could tell. "I just had a quick question, but it can wait."

"No." Sonora knew she'd been too eager. She forced herself to take a breath. "I mean, it sounds important. I'm sorry, Graham."

"Not at all. I can keep myself busy." He held up his book with a smile that melted through some of Sonora's fear and made her question if she should take the out or not.

"It was nice to meet you." She forced herself to take a step back. "Enjoy."

"Oh, I will." He smiled at them both and turned toward the chair next to the one she'd vacated earlier. Sinking in, he opened his book, and she watched the minute the world slipped away for him.

Yanking her attention back, she followed Blythe into the hall, questioning if she'd done the right thing. Could it have been so bad to talk about books with a handsome stranger?

FIVE

GRAHAM HAD READ the same paragraph three times, and it *still* made no sense. He closed the book and took a sip of his hot cocoa. Delicious and sweet, just as he liked it.

His mind formed the image of Sonora—also sweet, but beautiful and captivating, too. And young. Maybe too young?

He sighed and turned to look out the window into the darkness of the forest. Snow drifted gently down, illuminated by the outdoor lights. There was nothing more peaceful. He'd lived in Los Angeles so long he'd forgotten what it was like to see this much snow. He'd also forgotten what it was like to meet someone and not have them immediately know who he was.

She hadn't recognized him, had she?

He thought back to the look of utter shock on her face when he'd startled her. He almost laughed again but pressed his lips together. No, he'd read it on her face, surprise and embarrassment, but not recognition.

And what a relief that was. In fact, it was the whole reason he was here.

He searched his mind. Had he seen Sonora in the meeting? It would make sense that she was part of the group since Blythe knew her. He could recall the back of a blonde head a few rows in front of him at the meeting. It had matched Sonora's hair color.

He took a deep breath. This wasn't why he'd come to Vermont. He wasn't interested in finding another woman who, once she knew who he was, would manipulate him for what she could get out of him—or his bank account. He was done with that. Sure, Monique was beautiful—a model with aspirations for acting—but that beauty had turned out to be only skin deep.

The sweet cocoa slid down his throat, and he considered trying to read again, but he'd lost the taste for a fictional world when there was a puzzle to unravel in the present. Who was Sonora? Where was she from? What did she do for a living?

Does it matter?

Objectively, no, but if she was part of the retreat week, wouldn't that change everything? If she was as wealthy as he was, even at a younger age, there could be no fear that she was after him for his money. That thought was refreshing, and he almost jumped to his feet to find her, but common sense sobered him.

He'd invited her to sit, and she'd declined. Or had she? Blythe needed to speak with her so that was different than a flat-out no.

This time, he did jump to his feet before hesitating. It had been one day, and he still had the rest of the retreat. Would it look desperate if he went in search of her now?

The sound of wheels on carpet drew his attention to the hallway that led toward the lobby just as a familiar head of shaggy blond hair appeared.

"Marcus!"

"There you are." His friend looked haggard from a day of travel. His collared shirt was open, his tie hung askew, and his jacket was rumpled, a larger coat over his arm. "I'm never flying to Vermont again. You can't make me."

Graham laughed and slapped his friend on the shoulder, retaking his seat. "But you made it."

"Finally." Marcus slid into the seat Sonora had vacated and dropped his head back to the cushion. "It was awful coming in.

The turbulence was horrendous due to the storm. And then the car I'd hired couldn't make it so I ended up catching a ride in this truck with an older man who, while he was very kind, was hauling some sort of fish. Do I smell like fish? I think I smell like fish."

Graham laughed. "You smell fine. I'm glad you could make it, but I'm sorry about the bumpy road to get here."

Marcus sat up, rubbing a hand over his face, before he focused his gaze on Graham. "You're in an unusually good mood."

"Am I?"

"You are." Marcus leaned forward, skepticism on his boyish features. "What is it?"

"I don't know what you're talking about." Graham dropped his friend's gaze and studied the dregs of his hot cocoa.

"Come on. I've known you since grade school. You can't hide anything from me, and you know it."

Graham chuckled. "It's also the reason you work *for* me. There was no way I was going to let a competitor get to you."

"Don't butter me up unless you're going to give me a raise."

"Do you want a raise?"

Marcus rolled his eyes to the vaulted ceiling. "No, you pay me more than enough. Stop stalling Hast—" He cut himself off before spilling all of Graham's last name. "Sorry."

"I think we're alone." Graham looked around, again feeling the missed opportunity of a bookish conversation with Sonora. "I… met someone."

He hated how that sounded. How many times had he called Marcus up with those exact words only to find out months later the woman was only interested in his money, not *him*?

"Oh?"

"Well, kind of." He felt the need to backtrack. "Actually, not really."

"I'm confused."

Graham gave up and told his friend how he'd met Sonora.

"And you already pulled out the maple butterscotch hot chocolate? Things *are* serious."

"Stop it, Marcus." Graham ran a hand over his beard. "I only told you because you forced me to."

"Fair point. What are you going to do then?"

Graham had asked himself the same question and still didn't have a good answer. Maybe that *was* the answer. "Nothing."

Marcus lifted an eyebrow. "That does not sound like you, man."

"Maybe that's a good thing." Graham met his friend's gaze. "I feel like I've been on a dating treadmill that only ends up throwing me off every time. Monique was the last straw. I can't keep doing this to myself."

"I mean, I did warn you about that one." Marcus grimaced.

"I convinced myself she was different when, in reality, she was just the same as nearly every other woman I've dated. Selfish, self-focused, and money hungry."

"What about this?" Marcus waited until Graham met his gaze. "Try getting to know this Sonora woman."

Graham waited, but Marcus didn't add anything else. "And?"

"And nothing. Just let it, I don't know, progress naturally?"

Graham narrowed his gaze. "You do realize I'm only at this lodge for a week."

"If you still like her at the end of the week, you can exchange numbers or whatever, but just get to know her for who she is. I mean, that's the point of this week, right? To let go of the identity you're faced with on a daily basis and instead just be Graham. So let Sonora get to know Graham and see what happens."

Graham smiled. "And that's why I pay you the big bucks."

"Maybe I should take that raise." Marcus chuckled but grew serious. "Speaking of the thing we're not supposed to speak of, you're going to need to make a few calls."

"The sale?"

Marcus nodded. "The buyer is considering backing out."

Graham shot to his feet. "You should have led with that."

"I think this conversation was way more productive."

"How can you say that?" Graham felt tension creep back over his body. "You know how important this is."

Marcus stood and clapped him on the back. "I do, and that's why I know this is just a blip. I don't think they believed you'd take them up on their offer, and they were considering backpedaling. You just need to convince them it's the right choice. One call from you can allay their fears. I've got no doubt about that."

His friend's support meant a lot, but it didn't fully erase his worry. Tonight had given Graham a taste of what real life could look like for him, and it was intoxicating. He was going to fight to make his life less about work and more about this—real connections, real conversations—but that started with selling his company to the highest bidder and sloughing off the identity of CEO. If the sale didn't go through, that would never happen, and this glimpse of what life could be wouldn't matter.

Graham stood. "Come on. Let's go talk strategy."

SIX

"I'M SORRY, did I interrupt something?" Blythe wore the look of the cat who'd just caught the canary.

"I have no idea what you're talking about." Sonora nervously pushed a strand of hair behind her ear as she followed her friend and boss into the hallway.

Though she'd never admit it, her conversation with Graham had felt like *something*. He'd been so easy to talk to that she'd felt her guard drop. That fact alone sent warning bells clanging even as she suppressed a smile.

"It's just that you two looked so," Blythe searched for the word, "cozy."

"Can't two people have a conversation?" Sonora rolled her eyes.

"Yes, but that seemed…cozier." Blythe grinned.

"I'm not looking for cozy." Sonora averted her gaze. "What did you need?"

They stopped halfway toward the front desk near an elegant arrangement of poinsettias atop a mercury glass-topped table. Windows framed the opposite wall, and Sonora wrapped her arms around herself at the slight chill they put off.

"I'm sorry to pull you away from *nothing*, but there was an issue with your first paycheck processing. Something about your bank not recognizing the transfer?"

Sonora's heart leapt. "What?"

"I don't know what happened, but I thought I should tell you as quickly as possible."

The sound of two of the night staff members caused Sonora to look behind them. "Can we talk in your office?"

Blythe's eyes flooded with compassion. "Of course."

Sonora followed her friend the rest of the way out of the hall and into the spacious lobby with its two-story ceiling and myriad Christmas trees. The space always reminded her of the movies she watched as a kid. The ones that caused her to have dreams of greater things instead of her small life.

Once in Blythe's office with the door closed, Sonora sank into the same chair she'd claimed when she first arrived. "It's got to be Jonah."

Blythe lowered herself into the chair facing Sonora, and her brow wrinkled. "What do you mean? You broke up six months ago."

"Yes, but..." Sonora didn't want to get into her past. She wanted it to rest firmly there where her new life didn't have to be stained by it, but she'd left Louisiana a week and a half ago, and already he was clawing his way back into her present.

"I think he might have taken control of my account." She huffed out a breath. "I haven't really needed to buy anything since being here, so I wouldn't have noticed, but now I'm worried that inattention is going to be my downfall."

"Why would he have access to your account?" Blythe still wore the smart black pencil skirt and red collared shirt that made up the front desk staff uniforms during the holiday season, but she'd undone one button and let her hair down from the severe French twist she always wore it in. She looked more like the woman Sonora had known in college, and the truth came rushing out.

"I didn't know what I was doing, B. I mean, I did, but I didn't think something like this could happen to me." She was rambling, but she didn't know how to cut to the heart of it. "We got engaged about a year ago, but we'd been together for a year before that."

Blythe nodded. "I remember seeing your status change on Facebook."

"Yeah. I was happy at the time." Sonora pursed her lips. "When we got engaged, I was ready. You know I've wanted to be married, and at twenty-six, I thought it was finally time. Jonah had a good job as a criminal defense attorney and really seemed to love me."

If only she could go back to her younger self and shake some sense into her. To point at the red flags and warning signs she'd naively overlooked.

"Why do I sense a *but* coming?" Blythe leaned forward, elbows on her knees.

"Because the minute I said yes to marrying him, things changed. I didn't see it at first. I just thought he was excited to be married. He insisted we join our bank accounts, and he bought a house, using a large chunk of my savings."

"Without you knowing?"

Tears pooled in her eyes. "Yes. I—he said it was for us. He even forged most of the paperwork so it would be a surprise to me. He said he wanted me to have a nice place to live, and he moved me in as soon as he closed on the house. He said it was where we'd build our future."

"But it wasn't right?" Blythe's expression radiated compassion.

"It was the furthest thing from right. The house was more than I could afford on my own, but he assured me his job would provide the money for the mortgage."

"Effectively trapping you."

Sonora nodded. "I hate to admit how long it took me to realize what was going on. It was six months of him controlling every aspect of my life because he was *almost* my husband before I could see it." Her mind halted at the next part of her story. The part she couldn't bear to share—not even with a compassionate friend like Blythe.

"You have always looked for the good in people. It's not a negative thing, Sonnie."

"Maybe not, but it was my downfall in this case." She looked at her entwined fingers. "I finally woke up one morning and knew I had to get out of the whole situation."

"What did you do?"

"I packed a bag, took out the limit of cash from my account, and tried my best to disappear." Sonora recounted the first few days and how she'd looked over her shoulder at every turn. She knew she couldn't go to her friends' houses because everyone she knew thought Jonah was a good guy.

Jonah even had their friends at church convinced that *she* was the problem. She'd called up the wife of a couple they often hung out with and had asked to spend the night until she could get her bearings, but the woman had only insisted that she and Jonah just needed counseling and everything would be fine.

"I'm so sorry." Blythe's eyes held unshed tears.

"I finally called an older woman from my church. I'd stayed in a motel outside of town for a week and knew I couldn't keep paying out money like that since Jonah had frozen my cards. She was so kind and invited me to stay with her until I knew what I needed to do next."

"Oh Sonora, you could have come here."

"I did." Sonora smiled, looking up from her clenched fingers. "It just took a bit of time for me to sort out what I was feeling. Donna was great and gave me the time I needed. She lives out in the country, and I felt so safe there." *Or I did until he found me.*

"What happened to make you leave?" Blythe's shrewd gaze had caught on to something in how Sonora had answered. Her friend had always read her emotions so easily.

"He found me. I was running low on funds and risked using the only card I had left—my credit card—to take out a cash advance. I didn't think to go back into the city. I just did it at the small grocery store near where Donna lived. He got an alert and came to the house the next day. I guess he'd put two and two together."

"What happened?"

"He waited until Donna left for her volunteer position at the food pantry and confronted me at the house." Dread at the memory streaked through Sonora. "I wouldn't come outside but spoke to him through the storm door. I told him to leave, but he said he never would. He knew where I was, and he was going to come back every day until I realized he was right." She ran a shaky hand through her hair.

"Did he finally leave?"

"Only when Donna came back. I'd long since slammed the door in his face, but he just sat in his car, watching me." She shivered. "Donna told me I had to leave the state if I was going to be free of him, which is when I reached out to you."

"I'm so sorry. I feel awful though. You shouldn't be working. You should be relaxing and recuperating from that psycho."

Sonora shook her head. "No. I want to work. I may not have access to my finances anymore, but I'm not helpless. I wanted this job."

Blythe nodded. "Okay but know I'm here if you need a break or anything."

Sonora offered a thin smile but knew the casual telling of the story hadn't even touched the heart of what Jonah had done. His lies and manipulation had warped her in a way that frightened her. How was she ever going to trust again knowing how easily anyone could lie?

"I didn't mean to tease you about Graham," Blythe said.

Sonora looked up. "I know you didn't. I just don't know that I can trust a man again. I—" Her voice cracked, and the tears fell coursing down her cheeks. "I gave Jonah every ounce of love I had, and he returned it with lies."

Blythe got up and came to crouch on the side of Sonora's chair. She pulled her close into a hug. "Well, if there's one thing I can assure you of, it's that Graham Hastings is a good guy. *Shoot!*"

Sonora pulled back as her friend's body went rigid. "What's wrong?"

"I shouldn't have said that." Blythe covered her face with her hands.

"What? What did you say?" Sonora thought back over her friend's words, but nothing seemed out of the ordinary. "You mean he *isn't* a good guy?"

"No, it's not that." Blythe was full-on blushing now, red from root to tip, which made her freckles disappear. "*Shoot*," she repeated.

"B, what is going on?"

"Can we just pretend I didn't say that?"

"Say what?" Sonora's mind was already whirling through the possibilities. "Wait, you told me his last name. Is that it?" Her eyes narrowed.

"Nope. I definitely did not say anything." She pressed her lips together, eyes widening as if pleading with Sonora to agree with her.

"Hastings. That's his last name?" Sonora reached for her phone with a small but devious smile. She wanted to forget the last twenty minutes of spilling her ugly tale. She much preferred teasing Blythe about something she'd messed up—because Blythe Lockwood did *not* make mistakes.

"Do not Google his name, Sonora Lee Jackson!" Blythe stood up, ready to snatch Sonora's phone out of her hand.

"What is going on?" Sonora laughed, but it faltered at Blythe's expression.

They held each other's gaze for a long minute before Blythe finally sank into the chair facing her. Her eyes took in the closed door and then slowly made their way back to Sonora.

"If I tell you this, you have to double dog promise me that you won't say *anything* to *anyone*."

"Who am I going to tell?" Sonora almost laughed but it died on her lips.

"Seriously, Sonnie." Blythe looked sick to her stomach. "You can't tell the staff—you can't even tell Graham."

"You're kind of freaking me out. What, is he in Witness Protection or something?"

"It's worse than that." Blythe ran a hand down her face.

Worse? What was Blythe saying? She did tend to get dramatic at times, but her drama was undercut by a real current of worry.

"You know me, B. I won't say a word."

Her friend nodded. "I shouldn't tell you this, but you could just do a search and find out. At least this way you'll understand."

"Understand what?" Sonora was getting frustrated at Blythe's hedging.

"He's a billionaire."

Sonora wasn't sure what she'd been expecting, but it wasn't that. "What?"

She thought back to their interaction. He had been kind, not demanding as you'd expect someone with money to be, and his copy of The Sands of Salyea was worn and tattered. Couldn't a billionaire afford something nicer?

"But that's not the half of it." Defeat laced Blythe's words. "I might as well tell you all of it."

Sonora crossed her arms. "There's more?"

"This week is something my grandfather started a decade ago. It's called the Libertas Retreat, and it's a way for those with substantial wealth to come to the Lockwood Lodge to escape, essentially. They are only known by their first name and not allowed to talk about business, money, or their lives back home. It's supposed to be a type of reprieve. It also gives them a chance to get to know others like them but without the pressure. No posturing or comparison.

"Grandpa Archie says he got the idea for it when he went on a cruise once in Germany. No one knew who he was, and he found it to be the most liberating thing. It's even where he met my grandma." Blythe took a breath and smiled. "He's held it every year since. Well, up until last year."

"What happened?"

"Remember how you asked about my uncle?"

Sonora nodded.

"He messed up. It got out that a big tech mogul was coming and—let's just say it was a disaster and the last straw for Grandpa."

"That's how you got the job?"

"More or less. The week is by invite only and moves around each year so that no one can predict when the retreat will be. Grandpa put me in charge of this one in hopes that I could prove to him I'm ready for the responsibility of this job."

"Wow." Sonora took in the mystery behind it all with a wide-eyed stare. "And just *you* know about this?"

"Only LaToya and I know people's real identities. And now you. I—I'm in a huge breach of contract by telling you." Blythe bit her lip. "But you won't say anything, right?"

"Of course not." Sonora's mind still reeled with the details, but her silence was something she could assure her friend of.

"Is every guest this week a multimillionaire?"

"No. There are those that are part of the retreat, yes, though not everyone is *that* wealthy. But we'll also have regular guests coming for the holidays as well."

Sonora nodded. "Right. Well, it's just money." She gave a weak laugh.

But even as she said the words, her heart sank a little. While what she'd told Blythe was true—she wasn't looking for *cozy* or anything else—she couldn't help but think that Graham had been different. Or maybe that was just her hope?

But it didn't matter. He had more money than she could ever even imagine, and he'd never have struck up a conversation with her if he knew who she really was—a poor maid on the run from her ex-fiancé.

"Promise me you won't say anything," Blythe pleaded.

"I promise."

They locked eyes just as Blythe's cell phone rang. She picked it up and answered. "What's up, Hank?"

Sonora watched as color drained from Blythe's face, and she jumped up. "There's a problem at the pool."

SEVEN

GRAHAM SHIVERED as he wrapped a towel around himself.

"You just had to do laps while we worked things out, didn't you?" Marcus was fully clothed and perched at the end of a lounge chair in the indoor pool area.

"You know I think best when I'm moving."

"Oh, I know." Marcus stifled a yawn. "You negotiated that merger while on that hundred-mile bike race, and didn't you come up with our last digital product while running a marathon or something ridiculous like that?"

"Half-marathon." Graham corrected and used the edge of the towel to wipe his face. "You did call someone, right?"

"Yeah." Marcus shifted his attention to the door, but as Graham watched, his smile shifted to something wolfish. "Well, who do we have here?"

Graham turned, and there she was. Sonora entered the chlorine-scented pool area with Blythe right behind her. He tugged the towel more closely around him, wishing he'd taken a moment to pull on his shirt. It wasn't that he was embarrassed, far from it, but he hadn't expected two beautiful women to be the ones coming to the rescue at the pool. Wasn't there a maintenance man or something?

"Mr.—uh, Graham." Blythe looked flustered, and Sonora was doing her best not to look at him.

"Sonora, we meet again."

Her eyes jerked toward him, and he caught the faint tint of a blush at his attention. "Hello again." Her eyes dipped to his bare chest where the towel didn't cover.

He purposefully shifted focus to Blythe. "I'm pretty sure the drain is clogged. I…didn't expect you to answer this call."

She gave a half-hearted laugh. "Hank doesn't live up here. He's down in Middlebrook."

"That's who I got when I called." Marcus joined them. "Was that the wrong number?"

"No, it's perfectly fine. I'm just the only one here at the moment." She cast a dubious glance at the pool and back to Graham. "Perhaps I'll just close it for the night."

"It's definitely the main drain that's clogged." Marcus said. All attention snapped to him. "I worked as a pool boy for a few summers," he explained.

"Is there a way to fix it? Something I can do?" Blythe asked.

Marcus shot Graham a look. "If someone goes down there with a pool vacuum, yes."

"I'll do it." Now everyone looked at Graham. "I'm clearly the only one prepared for a swim." He looked back at Sonora. He'd caught her looking again, and his chest puffed out almost automatically.

He wasn't in as good of shape as he'd been in when he was in his twenties and thirties, but he made a habit of incorporating cardio and weightlifting into his daily routine. It paid off as long as he kept it up, and by the admiring look he'd caught before she looked away, Sonora agreed.

"I could change into a swimsuit," Blythe offered, looking at the pool with contempt.

"Please, don't worry about it. I'm happy to help." He turned to Marcus. "Walk me through it."

He did, and without much thought, Graham tossed the towel to the side and dove in. The water was blessedly warm, but the gargled sucking sound was louder now that he was in the water. It was definitely something wrong with the main drain like Marcus had thought.

Blythe unlocked the maintenance closet, and after Marcus messed around with a few things, he pulled out what Graham assumed was the pool vacuum attached to a rolling cart.

Taking the vacuum from Marcus, Graham cast one look up to the pool deck where three sets of eyes watched and then, with a little wave, dove down to the deepest part of the pool. Marcus had walked him through what to do, and it was easier than he'd expected. Soon, the sucking sound stopped, and he shot to the surface again.

"I think I got whatever it was."

Marcus knelt next to the pool with an ear to the water. "Sounds like it. Good job, man. But, uh, we need the vacuum back up here."

Rookie move, Graham.

Grimacing, Graham rolled his eyes. "Right. Be right back."

He caught Sonora's gaze one last time before he dove deep, and the memory of it followed him to the depths.

She was intriguing to him. He wanted to know more about her. What other books she liked to read, what kind of things she did for fun, what her favorite dessert was—anything that meant he got to have another conversation with her.

He latched onto the vacuum, his grip clumsy in the water that tried to pull him to the surface.

Was she like Monique though? The young woman, beautiful and talented though she was, had acted so differently when'd they'd accidentally met at a coffee shop. She'd run into him, spilling her coffee all over her coat, and they'd gotten to talking. Her beauty had stopped him at first, but it was the passion with which she'd talked about her aspirations for acting that had truly hooked him.

He was a sucker for passionate people. What was Sonora passionate about?

He got a good grip and pushed off the floor of the pool, lungs burning for air. He gasped in a breath and, with a few strong strokes, reached the ladder at the side of the pool. Marcus helped grab the machine, leaving Graham free to climb out.

Dripping water and shivering as his skin came in contact with the cooler air, Graham accepted the fresh towel from Marcus and met Sonora's gaze once again.

She looked down, to the dark windows behind him, and then to Blythe. What was she thinking?

"That should be fine until your maintenance man can look into it," Marcus assured Blythe.

"Thank you. And thank you, Graham. I truly don't know what I would have done. I'm sorry to interrupt your swim."

"Not at all. We were just doing some brainstorming." He introduced Marcus, mentally kicking himself for not doing it earlier. "He's my oldest friend and most trusted advisor," he added with a wink to Marcus.

"I'm just a sounding board, really." Marcus chuckled, and they all joined in.

Graham only had eyes for Sonora though. He was careful not to get too close to the women, as he was still dripping, wearing the towel as a cape now, but something had taken shape in his mind, and he wasn't sure he wanted to let it go. At least not yet.

"I hope we haven't spoiled your night," Blythe said. "Please let the front desk know if you need anything else."

"Will do," Marcus said for them both. He no doubt sensed Graham's indecision.

Instead of speaking up, Graham watched them both leave through the glass-fronted doors.

"Um, okay, who is *that?*" Marcus eyed him.

"Blythe Lockwood. She runs the resort."

"Not her. The one you were staring at. And who I might add, was staring back at you."

Warmth flooded Graham's chest despite his chills. "Really? She was looking at me?"

"Who is she?" Marcus' eyes narrowed.

"Sonora."

"Ah. Things are starting to click."

"I think I want to ask her out." The words tumbled out, and Graham wasn't sure if he regretted them or not. Was this another Monique situation, or was what he saw in Sonora something different?

"And?"

"It's a bad idea, right?" Graham ran the towel over his hair.

Marcus was unusually silent.

"What?"

His friend shrugged. "I stand by what I said before. Get to know her. It doesn't have to be anything high stakes. I know you like to *wow* women with all your adventurous date ideas but…why not ask her out to coffee?"

Graham opened his mouth to protest. He didn't just take women out to coffee. It was dinner at a Michelin star restaurant or a sunset cruise to Catalina Island on a yacht. He didn't do things like coffee dates because…

Why didn't he?

"You've got a worry line I'm not liking. What are you thinking?" Marcus pressed.

"Why not coffee?"

"That's what I said."

Graham had already turned toward his shirt discarded on a chair, but he heard more than saw Marcus roll his eyes to the wood-paneled ceiling.

"Maybe that's my problem." Graham pulled his shirt down over his still-wet hair. "Maybe I set too high of expectations." He rushed to the door leading into the hall.

"You're a genius," Marcus called over his shoulder.

The door opened with a squeak, and warm air rushed at him. There, down toward the end, he caught the sound of conversation and rushed in that direction. He skidded to a stop and took a calming breath before rounding the corner. The women stood together talking and both jumped when he appeared.

"Did something go wrong with the pool?" Blythe asked.

His gaze jumped between them but rested on Sonora. "No. I was wondering if I could have a word with Sonora. If you're not busy?" The words were ridiculous the moment they slipped out. It was nearing ten o'clock at night.

She finally looked up and met his gaze.

"Uh, yes. Sure. I'll…I'll see you tomorrow, Sonora." Blythe flashed a confused smile and disappeared down the hallway back toward the lobby.

He shifted back toward Sonora and caught the smallest hint of a smile on her lips. "I'm sorry—I didn't mean to interrupt."

She kept her gaze down. "Do you realize you forgot your shoes?"

"I—" He looked down. He was, indeed, barefoot in the middle of the hallway, water still dripping off of him. With a shrug, he said, "I wanted to ask you something."

She finally met his gaze, and his breath stalled. Her gray eyes deepened in the dim light of the hall, and a strand of blonde hair fell across her forehead. He watched as she pushed it behind her ear.

"What did you want to ask?"

She broke into his concentration. "Would you—do you like— I mean, do you drink coffee?" He slammed his lips shut. Had he completely forgotten how to function?

"I do." Her lips tightened, almost tipping to a smile.

"Is there—I mean, could we get—would you like to get coffee with me?" He ran a hand through his hair and came away with it dripping. Right, he probably looked a mess.

"Right now?"

He was fairly certain she was teasing him, but her guileless expression was hard to read.

"I was thinking maybe tomorrow. In the afternoon, perhaps? I heard there's a nice place in town." There, he was functioning again.

She hesitated, looking down the long hall. Did she think he was going to break their contract? He was about to reassure her that he wouldn't ask any off-limits questions when she answered.

"Sure."

"I—really?"

"Yes, but on one condition."

He held his breath. Didn't move.

"You wear shoes. There's a lot of snow out there." She turned and started off down the hall.

He was almost too stunned to reply, but when he did, it came with a laugh. "Meet in the lobby after lunch?"

"Perfect," she called out before she was gone.

He watched her disappear, dumbfounded.

He had a coffee date with Sonora.

EIGHT

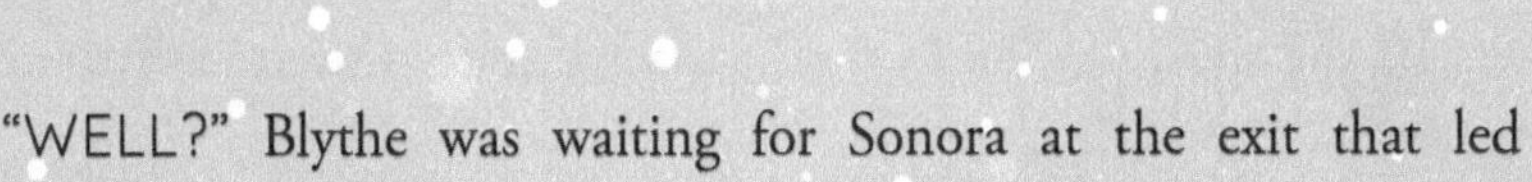

"WELL?" Blythe was waiting for Sonora at the exit that led toward her cabin.

"Are you stalking me?" At her friend's insistent stare, Sonora couldn't keep her smile in. "I'm going to coffee with Graham tomorrow."

Blythe's eyes bugged out. "No way!"

Heat flooded Sonora's cheeks, and she knew her friend saw it too. Her smile grew wider.

"Come on." Blythe grabbed her arm and pushed the door open.

A gust of frigid air hit Sonora in the face along with pin pricks of ice that forced her to dip her head. Blythe pulled her along under the covered path that led toward the employee cabins, but all Sonora could think of was the fact that she *really* wished she'd worn her jacket.

Sonora quickly swiped her band at the door, and the automatic lock showed a green light. Blythe pushed the handle down, and they both toppled into the warmth of the small space.

"I will never get used to this kind of cold." Sonora's teeth chattered.

"You'd be surprised." Blythe shrugged and rubbed her hands

up and down her arms but otherwise looked unaffected by their quick walk.

Sonora sought out the gas fireplace on the opposite side of the room and flicked the switch on. It was supplemental to the heating, or so Blythe had said, but she loved the atmosphere the flickering flames gave the space.

"I'm going to need you to tell me everything about what just happened." Blythe made herself at home, curling up in the armchair in the corner while Sonora slid to the floor in front of the fireplace.

Sonora stared into the gas flames. She wasn't sure what had come over her—or why she'd said yes. Perhaps it had been the bumbling way Graham had asked, the request so genuine. Or maybe she was just a fool for a handsome man who came to find her without even thinking to put on shoes.

"There—what's that smile about?" Blythe tossed a throw pillow at Sonora, who caught it and squeezed it to her chest.

"I don't know. Maybe I shouldn't go." Second thoughts flooded her mind. "I'm not in the right headspace to meet someone."

"What does that even mean?"

Sonora watched the flames dance and leap along the faux wood. "Remember? My guy-radar is off. Or maybe it's broken."

"Sonora." Blythe waited until Sonora met her gaze. "Just because Jonah didn't turn out to be who he claimed to be does *not* mean you're broken. You can't take on his mistakes."

"I should have known, B. Should have seen the red flags." Shame washed over her as she looked back on their interactions and how they should have sent her running.

Blythe shrugged. "I know people say love is blind, but I think it's different in this instance."

"How so?" Sonora craved her friend's honest assessment.

"Ever since I've known you, you've always been trusting, and I don't mean that in a naive way. You believe the best about people. You want to help them and can overlook a lot to see to the heart of someone. Maybe that's what happened with Jonah? Or maybe he was just really good at hiding the crazy."

She didn't know the half of it.

"What I'm saying is that Jonah was the one who lied. *He* was the one who misrepresented himself, and you are not at fault for believing the best in him." Blythe leaned forward, her hair falling around her shoulders and glowing a darker red in the firelight. "And you can't let him steal happiness from you."

Sonora frowned. "What do you mean?"

"What if Graham is the guy for you?" Blythe held her hands up, palms out. "I know, I know, you just met him, so I'm not *really* saying that. What I am saying is, hypothetically, if Graham—or any other guy—is the right guy for you, and you let this experience with Jonah rule you for the rest of your life, you'd be letting him steal your potential happiness."

An image of Graham at the pool flooded her mind. He'd instantly offered to help and had jumped in—literally—without complaint. His actions didn't sound like those of a billionaire who thought things like pool maintenance were beneath him. If what Blythe said about him was true and he had enough money to buy this resort without a second thought, he wasn't acting like it.

"I don't know." Sonora smashed her face into the cottony softness of the pillow and let out a deep breath. "He's a lot older than me."

"Does that bother you?"

Sonora frowned. Her mind supplied an image of the way his wet t-shirt clung to every shapely muscle of his sculpted chest and arms as if to add, *he's absurdly good-looking and you know it.*

"No, I guess it doesn't." What would *bother* her was if he was going to end up being a jerk like Jonah. Then again, she hardly knew Graham.

"Did he ask you to marry him?"

Sonora's head snapped up at her friends' off-the-wall question. "What?"

"Did Graham ask you to marry him?"

"No." Sonora laughed. The thought was too ridiculous to even consider.

"Then what's the big deal? You have coffee with him and get to know who he is without the pressure of things like his net worth. If there's something there, great. If not…well, at least you'll get a free cup of coffee from him. I'd go with the biggest size and all the bells and whistles. He can afford it." Blythe winked.

Sonora laughed at her friend's unique sense of humor. "You're serious. You think *I* should go to coffee with a *billionaire*?" She whispered the last word.

"Absolutely, yes."

"He doesn't even know I'm a maid." Saying the words out loud made the whole thing even more ridiculous. "B, who does he think I am? A billionaire too?"

"Who knows? Besides, does it matter?"

"Of course it matters. I barely have two pennies to rub together, and he's got, well—I don't know, but I assume it's a lot. I'm not billionaire dating material."

"Sonora, you're amazing. You're beautiful, smart, caring, and you love people. If he can't see that about you then you're better off without him, but you'll never know if you don't go."

❄

LATER, while Sonora lay in her bed staring at the wood-paneled ceiling of the small cabin, Blythe's words came back to her.

You'll never know if you don't go.

She knew why she'd said yes to Graham. He'd looked so unsure of himself, the complete opposite from how they'd interacted before, and it was so endearing she wanted him to relax. Wanted to give him what she could—and that was a yes.

Had her kindness won over her common sense?

She turned over on her side and stared into the flames of the fireplace. She hadn't meant to leave it on, but part of her mind knew she wasn't going to get any sleep. Not while she mulled over her hasty yes to the handsome man.

Sonora threw back the down comforter and padded to the mini fridge. There had to be something she could snack on. The dim light of the little refrigerator revealed an apple and half a peanut butter and jelly sandwich she wasn't sure the age of. *Ew.* She closed the door and went to the cupboard above the economy-sized sink. Nothing there but a packet of plain oatmeal and some English Breakfast tea.

Blythe had told her to stock up from the kitchen pantry where they had a section for residents of the lodge, but she'd forgotten to grab anything *good.* Her mood did not include oatmeal at the moment.

The clock showed a few minutes after midnight, and she warred with herself. Make the trek through the frigid snow to the kitchen or try to go to sleep? Her stomach growled, making the choice for her. To the kitchen it was.

She'd pulled on her coat, hat, and was reaching for her mittens when her phone buzzed on the table next to her bed. Curious who would be messaging so late, she picked it up only to drop it after reading the text preview.

(504) 555-7983: WHERE ARE YOU SJ?

Only one person called her SJ.
Jonah.

NINE

GRAHAM TURNED THE PAGE, anticipating one of his favorite space battle scenes coming up. He loved The Sands of Salyea and was so glad he finally had uninterrupted time to read it again in peace.

His phone rang.

Groaning, he was about to press decline when he read the contact name.

Father.

He groaned again, this time more pronounced, though he silenced himself. Marcus was in the room across the spacious sitting area in the suite he'd requested for them to share, and he didn't want to wake him. Marcus didn't know what it meant to slow down and had been going a mile a minute since he'd first told Graham about the potential issue with the deal.

Part of that is my fault.

Graham placed his bookmark between the pages, gently set the tome down on the side table, and pressed the accept button. His teeth ground so loudly they squeaked.

"You're selling VyCorp? To Rocky, of all people?"

Graham closed his eyes, the picture of calm—at least on the outside. "Hello to you too, Father."

"Don't change the subject. Why didn't you tell me about the sale?"

"Because you turned over our dying corporation to me years ago, and I'm not required to tell you my business decisions." He was narrowing in on impertinence, but he didn't care.

"The way I see it, I gave you an opportunity to prove yourself. Which you did. How can you throw that all away?"

"You taught me to make smart business decisions. This is that. I'm no longer satisfied as the CEO, and I want out. Rocky offered to buy, and I decided to take him up on the offer. He'll do right by my employees and is a smart guy, you know that."

"You're not thinking clearly, Graham. You've seen so much success. You can't just dump it because you're bored."

"I'm not bored. I'm burned out." *Not that you'd know the difference.*

"You're throwing away everything I worked for."

Was that a hint of hurt bleeding through his father's words? Impossible. "No, I'm choosing to make this decision for myself. Not that you'd care." He bared his teeth. He hadn't meant to say that, but it was too late now.

"You've got to be kidding me. Did I raise a businessman or a martyr?" his father scoffed. "What are you going to do? Cash in and move to the Bahamas? Come on, Graham, you're not an idiot. You start spending money like we both know you can, and you'll be destitute in five years."

Graham wanted to laugh. His father had no idea of his true net worth, and if Graham had his way, he never would. "I disagree."

"Of course you do, but don't forget *how* you got VyCorp. Without me—*your father*—you'd be nowhere."

Funny how you like to remind me in word but never in deed.

"I'm sure you won't let me forget that." Graham clenched his teeth again.

It would be too easy to fall into the trap Lawrence Hastings had set so perfectly. To give into the temptation to shout about his personal success, only for Father to claim all the glory for everything he'd taught Graham.

"A Hastings man never walks away, Graham. Is that what you're doing?"

Graham closed his eyes. "Is there something I can help you with, or did you just call to berate me about my choices?" *About a company you have no control over anymore.*

"I called to stop you from making a fool of yourself, but if you're not going to listen to reason, then I suppose we're done here." His father paused for a breath. "Just remember, Graham— we Hastings men have a reputation to uphold. You're nothing without money, so think long and hard about this decision. I won't be there to pick up the pieces once they shatter."

His father disconnected the call, but Graham sat there with the phone to his ear for nearly a full minute. Lawrence had a way of using words like a machete. He cut to the core and never looked back at the damage.

Jerking from his trance, Graham powered off his phone— something he almost never did—and shot to his feet. Book forgotten, he began to pace.

Words. That was all his father had given him, but it was more than enough to shatter his self-confidence when it came to the sale of his company. He knew it was the right decision, but that unshakable faith in his ability to make the right call was indeed shaking. How did his father still have that power over him?

Movement. Graham needed to do *something*.

Still tired from the laps he'd swam but not caring, Graham changed into running shorts and a lightweight t-shirt. The fitness center was open twenty-four seven, and he'd use that to his advantage. Run until he couldn't think. Couldn't debate with himself. Until all he wanted to do was fall into bed and sleep like the dead —they were the only ones who didn't dream.

The hallways were eerily quiet in the way that all places became after midnight when parties weren't the go-to event. He appreciated this fact. While he wasn't a partier, he had known his fair share of late-night events to schmooze a client or meet someone famous who loved what VyCorp did.

It was exhausting, all of it, but he'd done it. Done his job. And done it well. He'd grown the company back from bankruptcy since Lawrence had sold it to him. He'd improved the work environment, given raises, and increased vacation days—all things his father thought would sink them but actually proved to increase morale and therefore, productivity. It shot efficiency through the roof, and Graham had wanted so badly to accidentally-on-purpose send his father the year-end reports. He hadn't though.

Hastings men never bragged.

No, they just thought of themselves as more important than everyone else because of their money.

Graham made a fist. He didn't want to be that kind of Hastings, but he was always afraid it was creeping up on him. The sale meant astronomical profits for him based on his initial investment, and despite what his father thought, he was no longer that stupid kid who spent fifty grand on a nice meal to impress a girl.

Sure, he liked the finer things in life, it was true. But he always looked to Marcus as his compass. If his friend thought Graham was at risk of overindulging, he wouldn't do it. Thoughts of their earlier conversation only aided in reminding Graham that starting with a coffee date with Sonora was the right idea. It was exactly what he needed to normalize himself.

No more models. No more actresses. No more attention-seeking, selfie-taking, social media queens for him.

He picked up the pace and reached the main lobby. The night clerk was a bored looking young man who had his nose in his phone, thumbs flicking away. He was either texting or gaming, but either way, Graham didn't want to disturb the kid for directions to the gym.

It had to be past the lobby. He was almost certain, though Marcus would say Graham should never be in charge of directions, and it was true. Though a city like Los Angeles was one thing and a confined space like the resort was another. Surely, he could find the gym without too much trouble.

The hall narrowed, but there was no signage on the walls like most hotels. Normally, he would have seen signs for the business center and working space by now, but the lodge was more old-fashioned, like something you'd find in White Christmas. He liked that about it.

At the end of the hall, light spilled out through narrow windows in the doors, and he became even more convinced this was the gym. It made sense. It was out of the way, and it looked like a laundry room was off to the right.

He approached and looked through the narrow window. His movements halted. It wasn't a workout space. It was the kitchen. And Sonora sat on a stool at a stainless steel table with her head in her hands.

The sight twisted like a knife to the gut, and without thinking through what he was doing, he pushed the door open.

She screamed and nearly fell off her stool.

Quick reflexes honed by years of tennis threw Graham forward in time to steady Sonora before she could topple off the stool.

"We've got to stop meeting like this." He stood with an arm behind her back, so close he caught the scent of vanilla and cinnamon coming from her. Perhaps her shampoo? Or perfume?

"Graham. Hi." She righted herself the rest of the way on the stool and pushed her blonde hair behind her ears on the left side, leaving the right to fan down across her cheek. He caught himself before he reached out and pushed that side back too. It would be better to see her face, but he had *no* right to touch her like that.

Shaking himself from his thoughts, he took a step back. "I'm really sorry. I just—you looked..." He halted. What could he say? Devastated? Sad? Lonely?

"Pathetic?"

"No. I mean, you looked..." He still couldn't say bad. Not when he was staring into her eyes. Bad was the furthest thing from the words he'd use to describe her.

"It's all right. I'm just having a rough night." She motioned to the bowl in front of her where remnants of a chocolate mousse sat.

"Chocolate is a comfort food." He smiled, but she didn't return it, which caused concern to wrinkle his forehead. "Anything I can do to help?"

"I don't think so." She smiled. It wasn't bright, but it was genuine. "But thanks for offering. What are you doing here?" She looked down, and he remembered he was in his workout gear.

"I was looking for the gym." He rubbed the back of his neck. "I'm not great with directions."

She giggled, the sound soft and decidedly feminine. "It's on the other side of the resort. Do you want me to take you there?"

"No." He'd answered too quickly, but the thought of leaving her now that he'd found her again wasn't on his radar. "I mean, I really just needed to clear my head so a kitchen is just as good." He looked around, making a show of taking in the industrial kitchen.

"There's more mousse in the fridge. Or other fixings in the pantry." She motioned to the other side of the kitchen.

"Nah. That's okay." He shifted from one foot to the other.

"Do you cook?" she asked.

"I've been known to pull together a few things in my time." He sounded like a grandfather. What was he doing? But she laughed, and that was all he needed. "To be honest, my specialty is frozen pizza, PB and J's, or s'mores."

"That's quite the repertoire."

"You have no idea. And, wait for it," he held out his hands, "PB and J s'mores. Together."

She was laughing now, and the sound was at once soothing and captivating. It erased the memories of the conversation with his father and melted away the fears he had over the sale of his company. It didn't heal, but it did feel like a type of mending.

"I'm sensing a theme here."

"Oh?" He moved to the other side of the table, taking his own stool, but leaned forward to rest his elbows on the cold, stainless steel.

"You like to combine weird things."

It was his turn to laugh. "Maple and chocolate are *not* weird."

"Maybe not, but maple and butterscotch definitely are."

"You may have me there."

She dipped her head, pushing that same strand of hair back. He watched, his gaze transfixed by her slender fingers and the fact there was no ring there.

"What about you? Do you cook?"

Her gaze went to a far-off place before refocusing on him. "Yeah. I've been told I'm a good cook."

"What's your specialty?"

"Shrimp scampi."

His brows rose. "Impressive. You're not a chef, are you?" The minute the words slipped out, he knew he shouldn't have asked. It was job related and clearly on the no-no list. "Sorry. I guess anyone who can cook more than frozen pizza is a chef to me."

Worry pinched her forehead, and she stood. "I probably should get to bed." She picked up the bowl and deposited it near the sink.

"Sonora, wait."

She paused at the door, looking back at him through haunted eyes. Was she mad at him for asking? Did she think he was trying to snoop? The question came so naturally he hadn't thought about it, but he could see he'd put his foot in his mouth.

"Thanks for coming in here, Graham." She spoke before he could, softening her hooded expression with a real smile. "You helped make tonight better."

"Even after scaring you?" He offered a lopsided grin.

"Even then."

"You can call on me any time. Really." He poured as much earnest honesty into his expression as he could and was rewarded with a blush. "See you tomorrow?"

She paused at the door, her back to him, and he wondered if she was rethinking their coffee date. His abs clenched as he sent up a silent prayer she wouldn't. He wanted to see her again. To make her laugh again if at all possible, because there was something fragile about the woman that made him want to protect her. Not in a macho way, but in a way that reminded her she wasn't alone. He wanted to stand by her.

"Tomorrow." The word was a whisper, but he clung to it in the silence of the kitchen as she slipped out into the hallway.

Graham wasn't sure what was happening to him. He was the furthest thing from impulsive, that wasn't a trait a CEO had the luxury of, but Sonora made him want to see what life could be like if he seized the more impulsive side of himself and let it show him the way.

TEN

SONORA WIPED down the sink counter, the pungent cleaning spray permeating the air. She coughed, doing her best not to take in deep breaths, but it was difficult in the small space. Not for the first time, she wished the bathrooms had stronger fans, but they were the kind that came on with the light and hardly seemed to do anything.

She bent down and picked up a pile of dirty towels and took them over to her cart to dump them in the appropriate bin. It had been a week and a half of work, but she was getting into the rhythm of it. Being a maid was a far cry from her human services degree with a minor in global studies, but at this point, anywhere that was as far away from Jonah as she could be was a good thing.

She shivered, thinking of the text she'd gotten from him the night before. The one that had sent her to the kitchen and to another unexpected meeting with Graham. She'd almost accused him of stalking her, but it was clear from his expression that he hadn't expected to see her there.

It was odd though, the way he'd so easily put her at ease and how his humor lessened the tension she'd felt because her ex had already found her new number. She was simultaneously glad and also nervous that she'd agreed to have coffee with him. How was she supposed to spend a whole hour—or longer—with the man and not admit to him *who* she really was?

It was one thing to meet up here and there at the resort, but to sit across from him at a café and not put his assumptions to rights felt wrong. Or did she only assume he didn't know that she was a maid? She bit her lip as she tossed the contents of the half-full trashcan into a larger bag attached to her cart. Who did he think she was?

Her wrist buzzed, and she frowned, looking down at the cuff. Blythe was summoning her. Sonora laughed at the thought but tapped the bracelet once to signal she'd received the message.

After one final check around the room, Sonora rolled her cart out into the hall and headed toward the lobby. Halfway there, she stowed the cleaning cart in one of the closets meant for them and went the rest of the way on her own, per the instructions she'd gotten from Dominique.

No carts in guest areas, except for rooms.

She understood the rule. No one wanted to see a laden house-keeping cart in the middle of the lobby. But she also saw the allure of leaving it behind on the off chance she ran into Graham. Her stomach fluttered with nerves at the thought, suddenly glad she'd worn her favorite burgundy sweater and light-wash jeans.

Unlike other hotels she'd stayed at, the Lockwood didn't have any clothing regulations for the housekeeping staff other than clean-looking. She'd pushed back, sure that Dominique was joking, but the woman had only shaken her head and smiled, explaining that Mr. Lockwood—Blythe's grandfather—had wanted to keep the charm of the place. He insisted on hiring from Middlebrook to provide jobs to the small town and had offered them the chance to feel at home at the resort, despite the fact they were *serving*. It was the term Dominique had used.

Sonora stepped from the hall into the lobby area, and her tension seeped away. Graham wasn't there. In fact, there was only one older woman reading by a window, and she didn't move an inch when Sonora walked past.

"You wanted to see me?" She popped her head into Blythe's office.

"Ah, yes. Here," she held out an envelope to Sonora.

"What is it?"

Blythe quirked an eyebrow, which Sonora took to mean, *open it and see.*

She did and blinked. "A check?"

"It's your wages. I told you there was an issue with your bank, so I figured I'd just go straight to the source. I thought maybe you could create a new account at the local bank in Middlebrook rather than rely on past accounts."

Sonora gasped at the amount. "This can't be right."

"It is." Blythe looked back to her laptop, ignoring Sonora's questioning stare.

"B, I don't want charity."

"And you're not getting it." Blythe met her gaze straight on. "We pay well—another part of my grandfather's stipulations. I'm more than happy to carry on the tradition."

Sonora looked back at the amount. It would more than cover her student debt payments. A few months of this, and she could afford to fix her car and maybe find a place to live in town. A few months past that, and she would actually feel like she had her feet under her.

"Thank you."

"Don't thank me," Blythe laughed. "You're doing the work. You've earned this."

Sonora tucked the check into her jeans pocket and was about to go when she had a thought. "Could I borrow your car?"

Blythe looked up. "Of course. Why?"

She loved that her friend accepted and *then* asked questions. "I want to drive myself to the...coffee meeting today with Graham and Wilma won't make it."

"The date, you mean?" Blythe grinned.

"I'd like to go down early and maybe set up an account at the bank like you said."

"Fine by me." Blythe reached into her desk and plucked out a set of keys. "Here. Take them now. I hardly leave the resort these days." She let out a sigh, and Sonora made a mental note to make time to sit down and talk with Blythe when it wasn't during business hours. It was clear her friend was overworked and perhaps tired, but was she also lonely?

"Thanks." Sonora took the keys and pocketed them. "But B, I'm kind of having second thoughts."

Blythe turned her full attention to Sonora. "About the job?"

"No. The…date. I feel wrong not telling Graham who I am." *And what I'm not.*

"You're a beautiful woman he met at a resort. What more does he need to know? You can tell him about where you're from if you like."

Blythe spoke matter-of-factly, but Sonora didn't think it was that cut and dry. She'd agreed to have coffee with the man which, while it wasn't a marriage proposal like Blythe had said, it wasn't *nothing* either. If this was the beginning of anything, even a simple friendship, and she started out by lying to him—

"He's not going to be talking about who he is either. You'll both be keeping things—your pasts—separate from the moment because that's the beauty of this week."

"But he's going to assume I'm wealthy since that's the point of the retreat, right?" It made her skin crawl to have him think she was one thing when she was the complete opposite.

"I won't betray any more than I already have, but there are a few others here that don't have billions to their name."

"B." Sonora saw her friend's thinly veiled attempt for what it was, exploiting a technicality to make Sonora feel better and to cover up for her own mistake of sharing when she shouldn't have.

"You can't tell him, Sonora." Blythe's expression turned grave. "I know this goes against the friend code, but I have to swear you to secrecy. After signing the NDA, I could get in *major* trouble if it got out. I mean, he could shut this place down with a snap of his fingers if he wanted to."

Sonora frowned. That didn't sound like something Graham would do, but she didn't really know him, did she? She considered both sides to the argument—if he was the good guy she thought him to be, telling him the truth wouldn't truly endanger Blythe's job. Then again, she didn't know much more than that he liked to create odd culinary combinations and he read space operas for fun. That wasn't enough information to go on if she was going to be risking Blythe's career.

It was Blythe's pleading look of desperation that finally pushed Sonora over the edge. "Fine. I won't say anything."

"Thank you, thank you, thank you." Blythe's hands pressed together like she was offering up a prayer of thanks.

"Don't be dramatic." Sonora grinned.

"I just started this job—I can't lose it after one month. Plus, I don't think you have anything to worry about. If things go well with Graham, he's not going to care if you have a hundred million or five dollars to your name. And if he does, then clearly he's not the right guy for you."

Blythe's kind words were a good reminder even if Sonora still had her doubts. It was possible this was the first and last date she'd have for a long time. Either way, she was going to Middlebrook this afternoon to meet with the handsome man she couldn't quite stop thinking about.

ELEVEN

TO SAY he was a little disappointed would be an understatement. Graham had arrived in the lobby a few minutes before the time he'd arranged to meet Sonora, and she wasn't there. He'd waited, wondering if he should ask the front desk to ring her room, but then Blythe had found him, offering a warm smile.

Her explanation that Sonora was already in town had come like a blow, but she'd assured him Sonora was sorry she couldn't give him the news in person. Something had come up. At least she was planning on meeting him there and hadn't ghosted him on purpose. Or so he told himself.

He'd accepted Blythe's offer of a driver who often shuttled guests to Middlebrook, and now they were arriving at the outskirts of the quaint town that looked like the inspiration for a Christmas card.

Everywhere Graham looked, he saw green garland, red ribbon, and oversized ornaments. They gilded the storefronts, hung over doors, and twisted up light poles. If he didn't know better, Graham would have thought he'd arrived at the North Pole.

"Is it always like this?"

The driver glanced into the rearview mirror. "Like what?"

"So festive?"

"Oh yeah." The older man grinned "We go all out for Christmas. And that's the café, sir." The driver nodded across the street as he pulled up in front of what Graham assumed was a post office, though it was hard to tell with the six-foot candy canes flanking the door.

"Thank you." He tried to hand the man a tip, but he just shook his head.

"Merry Christmas, sir."

Not used to people refusing his money, Graham returned the sentiment and then stuffed the fifty into his pants pocket before climbing out. Cool, crisp air hit him with a bracing gust, and he immediately flipped up the collar of his peacoat. Why hadn't he brought a scarf too?

Digging his hands into his pockets, he did a slow turn, observing the snow lined street. The town continued on for a few more blocks to his right. He thought he caught sight of a sign for a grocery store, a small Mexican restaurant, and a barber shop. The parking lot between the shop and an old school movie theater had been turned into a mini Christmas tree lot stacked with fir and pine trees. The numbers were thinning, but Graham assumed that was only natural with Christmas a little over a week and a half away.

To his left, he caught sight of a beauty shop, hardware store, print shop, and another small parking lot half-filled with vehicles. His eyes traveled from there across the street to his destination. The Grind, a café and gift shop which was clearly *the* attraction of the town and its visitors. It was sprawling, nearly taking up the whole block, and he could see the distinct sections devoted to coffee, food, and gifts.

He cast a glance up and down the street before side-stepping the mound of snow at the curb and lightly jogging across to the cafe. The rich aroma of coffee greeted him while he was still feet away, and he grinned. There was nothing like a good cup of coffee, especially when it was this cold.

He stepped inside and sniffed. His nose was already running

from his brief stint outdoors, and he patted his jacket. He regretted not stuffing a tissue into his pocket. Maybe there was a restroom somewhere—

His thoughts slowed when he caught sight of Sonora.

She sat across the crowded room at a small round table toward the front of the shop where a floor to ceiling window looked out to the street. She sat with her hands in her lap, leaning over a paper on the table.

As he watched, a man shuffled up to her. Graham's eyes narrowed instantly at his disheveled appearance. He wore once-white tennis shoes and a stained down jacket over ratty jeans. His beard wasn't trimmed, and every inch of his exposed skin was covered with wrinkles and the sun-worn skin of someone who spent most of their life outside.

Graham took several steps forward but stopped when Sonora grinned up at the man. Graham watched and observed her body language. She was relaxed and open, clearly at ease and inviting the man to talk. Her forehead wrinkled, and he took another step, but as he drew closer, he could tell she was merely empathizing with him.

She leaned down and pulled up her purse where she rifled inside and came up with a couple of twenties that she handed over. To Graham's surprise it looked as if the man was trying to give her back some of the money, but she waved him off.

Generous to a fault.

Graham's brow dipped. No, that wasn't right. That sounded like his father.

The older man shuffled off, and Graham took the opportunity to cross the room. "Hi."

Sonora looked up and returned his smile. The mere sight of it eased any tension he'd felt when he first saw her alone.

"Was he bothering you?" Her smile clouded over with a frown, and he clenched his jaw. Why had he led with that?

"Not at all. He asked about some coffee, and I was happy to help him buy some."

Forty dollars would buy more than coffee. Graham thought of the fifty in his pocket—would he so easily give it away to a vagrant?

"I see." Graham sat without her consent and felt that as another misstep. "Sorry, may I sit?"

The warmth returned to her eyes. "Of course. We had a meeting." She'd hesitated, and he wondered if she had wanted to call it a date.

He wanted to. "Can I order you a drink?"

"I thought we could look together. I haven't seen the menu yet."

"Perfect." He slipped out of his jacket, glad for the thick flannel overshirt Marcus had insisted he put on over his long-sleeved shirt. He hadn't thought he'd need it, but even the cafe, which had seemed warm at first, didn't reach to the cold in his core from mere minutes outside.

He followed Sonora toward the counter but found his gaze returning to her profile more than the menu. The soft lines of her cheeks and the pink of her lips caused a different kind of heat to flare in his chest.

"What?" She sent him an inquiring look.

"Nothing." He shifted his focus back to the board. "Do you know what you're going to get?"

"I think it's between the peppermint mocha and the maple chai tea."

"I hadn't seen that one." In truth, he hadn't seen anything. His eyes traveled over the artfully handwritten menu board, but he couldn't seem to process the words. His thoughts were trapped by the beautiful, kind woman next to him.

"What can I get you?" The barista asked. She flashed a bright smile at Sonora and him in turn.

"I think I'll go for the peppermint mocha," Sonora said.

"Good choice," the woman said. She wore dark-rimmed glasses, and her long, highlighted blonde hair twisted in a braid over her shoulder. Her name tag read Penelope.

"Well, Penelope," he nodded toward the tag, "it's my first time here. What do you suggest?"

"Coffee or tea?" His question didn't faze her one bit.

"Coffee."

"Hot or iced."

"Hot." He frowned.

"Don't look at me like that." She grinned. "Some people still order cold drinks. And do you like sweet or less sweet drinks?"

"Sweet."

Penelope grinned. "That's all I need to know."

He blinked, but his smile surfaced instantly. "I like your style, Penelope. Merry Christmas." He slid across his black debit card and tossed a fifty-dollar bill into the tip jar.

"The drinks will be right up." She noticed the tip and nodded approvingly. "A *very* Merry Christmas to you."

He caught Sonora's smile as they returned to the table. "What do you think your drink will be?"

"Hopefully something good." He allowed some of his nerves to come out in a low chuckle.

"Thanks for the drink."

He blinked. "What?"

"For paying. For the drink. I appreciate it."

"I—uh, sure." He swallowed his surprise. When was the last time any woman had thanked him for something as trivial as coffee? A trip to Paris? A diamond tennis bracelet? Sure, but not a cup of coffee.

"That was a generous tip."

"It was nothing."

She turned to look at him. "Yet you didn't approve of what I gave Jerry."

"Who's Jerry?"

"A veteran and a volunteer at the local church."

He searched his memory for who she could be talking about.

"The man you saw me talking to when you walked in. His name is Jerry."

Light dawned, but he felt his brow wrinkle.

"What's that look mean?"

"What look?" He schooled his features.

"The one that says you disapprove of me giving money to Jerry, but you think it's fine to leave a fifty-dollar tip at a coffee shop." She challenged him with a raised eyebrow and a smile.

"I don't disapprove." Though, as he said the words, he wondered if they were true. "It's just that I'm from Los Angeles, and we've got a big homeless population there. I see the problem, I really do, but I've found it's more effective to put money into programs that are proven to help those in need instead of throwing money at every person who asks." He winced. That had come out harsher than he'd intended.

"I agree that a lasting impact often comes through organizations like you mentioned, but I don't think it's the only way. I think there are times when, on a case-by-case basis, you're meant to give to someone in need. Jerry only asked for a dollar to get some coffee, and I had more to give, so I did."

Graham watched as compassion flooded Sonora's eyes. She was passionate about this, and he could see it written on every earnest line of her face. There was something deeper here for her.

But before he could say anything, the barista caught his eye. "Hold on. Let me get our drinks."

She nodded, and he turned to the bar, his thoughts colliding. This conversation felt dangerously close to the topics he tried to avoid on most first dates, but Sonora didn't appear angry. Just passionate.

"Here you are." The barista slid the drinks toward him. "One peppermint mocha and one malted maple latte."

He searched the board.

"It's from the secret menu." Penelope tapped her temple with a grin.

"I'm sure I'll love it. Thanks." He flashed a smile, but he knew it looked how he felt. Distracted.

Retracing his steps, Graham set the drink in front of Sonora and slid back into his seat. He took a sip to give him an extra moment to think. Steer the conversation away from the homeless or dig in to why Sonora was so passionate about this topic?

Flavors assaulted his tastebuds, and his eyebrows rose. "Wow. That is so good." He sent a thumbs up to Penelope, and she nodded knowingly, before turning back to Sonora. "I'm sorry. It's none of my business who you donate to or how."

She observed him thoughtfully, taking a sip before placing her drink on the table between them. Her gaze dropped to it, and he wondered what she was thinking. How she'd respond.

"I hate to see anyone in need. Some say it's a weakness, but I think it's a strength. I know I can't save anyone by giving them money, but if I can help influence one person's circumstance, no matter how briefly, that's enough."

The tightness in his chest loosened. "I think it's easier to walk past someone in need when I know I'm donating toward a cause. I hate to admit that."

"Don't." She reached out and lightly squeezed his hand before drawing hers back. "It's honest. That's the place to start."

He straightened, more affected by her gentle words and light touch than he could have imagined. Who was this woman who spoke with such passion about the needy? What did she do—

He cut the thoughts off with the chop of a mental axe. None of that mattered this week. In reality, it didn't matter at all, but it was a good reminder of the agreement he'd signed.

"So…what's your favorite food?"

She laughed, his intended response, and took another sip of her drink. "I'm sorry. I go too deep sometimes." Her cheeks flushed, and she looked out the window.

"Don't apologize." He waited for her to meet his gaze. "I like deep."

The blush deepened and caused his heart to do flips in his chest. There was a connection with Sonora that had been lacking in his past relationships. Those women were stunning, but most cared more about themselves than anything else—sometimes even him. It had taken him an embarrassingly long amount of time to recognize that with some of them and less time with others, but it was refreshing to sense something different with Sonora.

She offered a type of raw honesty he'd craved. The kind of qualities he had always wanted to see in the woman he was dating. And he was going to call it that—a date—because he hoped it wasn't too soon to wish it would be the first of many.

TWELVE

THE FRIGID AIR cooled her warm cheeks as Graham held the door open. He'd suggested a walk, and now she slipped her hands into a pair of gloves he'd insisted on buying for her. He was going above and beyond, or so it seemed, but she couldn't help but think that a coffee and gloves didn't even register to him as money spent. Not when he had billions in the bank.

She ducked her head into the folds of her scarf and blew out a breath to warm her nose. She couldn't be thinking about things like that. It wasn't fair to him that she knew more than she should. And he wasn't flaunting his wealth. He'd been genuinely concerned about her hands in the cold air. He'd even bought a scarf for himself.

A quick glance over at Graham showed he was strolling ahead without a care in the world, taking in the sights of the small town in a relaxed manner. The navy scarf wrapped around his neck created a rakish appearance, but it worked for him.

Everything about Graham was different than Jonah.

She winced at the thought. She didn't want to compare her ex-fiancé to Graham, but she couldn't help it. Where Jonah was controlling and quick to argue, Graham seemed relaxed and wary of offense. She barely knew him, but she was drawn to the handsome man and his ability to be honest with her. Or, as honest as their situation allowed.

But there was still the small fact that he had no idea about who she really was. What would this handsome billionaire think of going on a coffee date with a maid?

A blush creeped onto her cheeks again, but this time, it was from shame. She hated not telling him the truth. If—and it was a *big* if—there was something sparking between them, it wasn't fair for him not to know.

Their boots crunched on snow as they passed a boutique with women's clothes on display. Sonora couldn't help the way her head turned to take in one of the dresses. It was red velvet with lace sleeves and made Sonora imagine an elegant ball. It looked much too fancy for the small town, but she appreciated it anyway.

"You'd look good in that."

Sonora's eyes widened, feeling guilty that she'd been caught looking. "What?"

"The dress. Sorry, I thought I caught you admiring it."

"It's nice." She kept walking, and he followed. They passed a few tourists bundled up in thick winter coats, and Sonora began to sense the weight of their silence. Was he regretting asking her on a walk?

"Penny for your thoughts?" She hazarded a look at him, not sure what else to say.

He smiled back, his manner relaxed. "I was thinking that it's nice to be able to walk at a slow pace."

"You said you were from Los Angeles. Is it really crowded there? Always busy?"

"Definitely. Not to mention the traffic." He shook his head.

"I understand traffic. I'm from just outside of New Orleans. It's crowded there too."

"I can imagine." He nodded as they walked past a bookstore and reached the edge of a large park. "Is that an ice rink?"

She moved to look past him. "It is. Do you skate?"

"Not if I want to stay on my feet."

"Me either."

They shared a laugh, and he nodded toward a snowy path. "Care to walk around the park, or are you getting too cold?"

She was chilled, but not teeth-chattering cold yet. "Let's do it."

The trees that lined the path were wrapped with white Christmas lights that glowed despite the light of day. Sonora could only imagine how magical it would look at night. A twist of her heart reminded her that she could find out any time she wanted. This was her home now.

"My turn. What were you thinking about?" Graham's voice cut into her thoughts.

"Not much." She certainly couldn't share what she'd *just* thought. "I mean, you did catch me looking at the dress."

"That's it?" His eyes narrowed as if he were searching for her honesty.

"That and…" She hesitated. She couldn't admit she lived here now, and there was also no way she'd admit she'd been comparing him to her ex. "I guess I was wondering what brought you here."

He bobbed his head from side to side. "Hard to know what I can share. You know." He gave her a look that she interpreted as him trying to decide what he could and couldn't share under the agreement Blythe had told her about.

"Mmmhmm," was all she said.

"Without getting into the details, I would say that I'm here in Vermont because I wanted a break. Or maybe it was more that I *needed* one. I'm on the edge of something big at work."

He shot her a glance as if worried he'd said too much, but she merely nodded.

"If all goes well, I'll be free to do what I want to. The thought of that is both tempting and terrifying."

"What do you want?"

"Um." He rubbed at the back of his neck and offered her a sheepish look. "I don't know."

She laughed but tamped down her amusement when his shoulders slumped. "I'm not laughing at you. I promise. I just expected you to have it all laid out. You seem like a very organized person."

"Usually, I am." They turned the corner, and screams rent the air as a group of kids all fell on the ice in one big, snow-coat-wearing pile. "But part of me wonders if I don't need true freedom to be able to figure it out."

"Like a life-pause?"

"More like a life change." His gaze trailed across the blindingly white ice before coming back to rest on her. "That sounds dramatic, but I was born into…responsibilities. Probably like a lot of people here this week. I'd like time away from the weight of that to dig into what *I* want."

"What would you do if you could do anything?" Sonora dug her hands deeper into her pockets, the plush softness of the new gloves not quite enough to warn off the chill.

"I wish I knew. But I do know one thing." He paused near an evergreen-covered arch that led to the ice rink. "I want to do something that matters."

His eyes met hers, sending warmth swirling in her stomach at the intensity she saw there. She dipped her head and turned back to the path, sensing his gaze following her.

Here was this billionaire in a life crisis telling her he wanted to do something that mattered. She could think of a thousand ways the money he spent on a haircut could go to help those less fortunate. The thought of his wealth was staggering, but it wasn't like she understood it. Or the responsibilities that came with that type of money.

He wanted a change. She'd been forced to take one. Everyone had their own problems to live with and work through, didn't they?

Sonora stopped in her tracks.

"Sonora, are you all right?"

She kept her back to him. She needed a minute to school her features. "I'm fine."

"Did I say something wrong?"

Composed, she turned to face him. "No. I was just thinking about what you said. That's a good desire. Honorable."

"What about you?" He took a step closer, his cologne invading her senses and causing her thoughts to scatter.

"What about me?"

"What would you do if you had no restrictions? No limitations?"

A million ideas raced through her mind, but one rose to the surface. "Travel."

His brow furrowed. "Anywhere specific?"

"Everywhere." She moved to walk past him, needing space, but her well-worn boots, more for fashion than utility, slipped on an icy patch.

Her feet flew out from under her, and she was certain she was about to hit the ground—hard—when a strong hand gripped her arm, steadying her.

"Be careful. That could have been bad."

Graham pulled her close against him as she worked to regain her footing.

Of all the times to trip, it had to be now. "Thanks."

Sonora's feet stabilized, but he didn't pull away. "Are you good?"

"Yes." She made the mistake of looking up. The sharp line of his jaw, covered by close-cropped, dark brown hair flecked with gray, was at her eye level. His lips quirked up in a smile and she raised her eyes to meet his. Brown threaded through with gold. Like sunlight through a forest in winter.

Was it her imagination, or had he pulled her a little closer?

"Sonora," he began.

She came to her senses in a rush and pushed against him. He instantly let her go, though his hand extended in case she slipped again. His close proximity had fuzzed her mind. She needed space to regain some semblance of coherent thought, but her emotions rebelled. They wanted her close to enjoy the protection of a man like Graham.

A man she hardly knew.

"I should probably start heading back. I parked by The Grind."

"May I walk with you?"

Another thud of her heart at the fact he didn't presume he could accompany her. Who was this man, and how was he not married?

The thought stopped her cold. "You're not married, are you?" The words tumbled out.

"What? Married? No." He looked momentarily affronted. "I'm definitely single."

How is that possible?

They turned down a sidewalk bathed in sunlight, and Sonora was more confident that she wouldn't trip again. "Sorry. I'm just surprised."

"At?"

"That you're not taken." She couldn't hide the heat flaming her cheeks this time and caught Graham's rapt attention on her face, a glint of humor in his eyes.

"A shock to all, I'm sure." He chuckled. "I spend a lot of time working. Too much time. And now I've hit my forties with not much to show for it."

She read between the lines. He had money—that much was clear—but perhaps that wasn't something he valued as much as she'd initially thought.

"I see."

He stopped. "Wait. Are you married?"

"No." Her adamant response landed heavily between them, leaving space for a modicum of truth from her. "I was engaged to be married but…we ended it." She didn't know what else to say.

"Did you end it or him?"

Sonora drew in a breath. "I did. He wasn't the man I thought he was."

Silence threaded around them like the chill wind, but Sonora found it was companionable. For as confident and poised as

Graham was, he wasn't intimidating. At least not like she'd thought he would be.

"I'm sorry." He looked to be composing the rest of his thought. "I know how that feels. I've dated quite a few women who have turned out not to be who I thought they were as well."

"Quite a few, hmm?" Sonora took the easy out with humor, but she was rewarded by his smile.

"Oh yes. I'm a hot commodity." He pretended to preen. "Nerdy guy who likes to read space opera and high fantasy and dresses up for Comic-Con. Apparently, it's a winning combination."

Sonora laughed. "You do *not* dress up for Comic-Con. Do you?"

"I'll never tell."

The warmth from earlier coursed through her again, edging out her worries. It didn't mean they weren't still there, but they paled in comparison to the brightness of Graham's smile.

THIRTEEN

SONORA'S LAUGH WAS INTOXICATING. He'd admit to all of his nerdiest tendencies if it meant hearing it again.

"Have you ever been to Comic-Con?"

"No." There was that laugh again.

"Don't knock it 'til you've tried it. It's a lot of fun."

They were passing the boutique again, and his eye caught the red dress Sonora had gaped at. The reaction had surprised him, but he would have done the same thing for a vintage Rolex. His opinion held—she would look amazing in it. He had to hold back the urge to march into the shop and plead with her to let him buy it for her.

Not that she needed him to buy her things. Not if she was at this retreat. Still, the idea slowed his steps.

"I'm sure it's fun. I've just never had the chance to go."

He sped up to catch her. He didn't want the date to end, but the parking lot was only half a block away. The scent of coffee swirled around them again, and he considered getting a second cup of the amazing concoction Penelope had created, but he was fairly certain Sonora wouldn't go for another. She seemed determined to get back to the Lodge.

"Hey, where would you go if you could fly anywhere tomorrow?"

His random question drew her up just as they came to the end of the coffee shop. "Anywhere?"

"Anywhere."

Her nose scrunched as her eyes searched the blue sky for her answer. He caught sight of a smattering of light freckles across the bridge of her nose and cheeks.

"Africa."

He opened his mouth to reply at her shocking answer, but she cut him off. "No, India. Or…maybe Russia? Or, I mean if we're talking *anywhere*, then New Zealand. I mean, it is where they filmed Lord of the Rings."

Graham thought his face might split. "You like Lord of the Rings?"

"Who doesn't?" She took a step back, her keys in her hand now.

Is that a sign? Do I need to back off?

"Thanks for today. This was fun." She took another step backwards, and he took one toward her. He caught sight of a black Lexus SUV behind her. She had nice taste in cars.

"Sonora, I know we just met but…" He trailed off. He was starting to sound like a badly written rom-com. "Would you want to do something tomorrow, maybe?"

"What do you have in mind?"

His heart leapt that her response wasn't no. "I—I don't know, but I can figure something out."

She looked down at the keychain as she fiddled with it. "Can I let you know?"

His spirits drooped some. "Sure. Of course." He tried to hide his true feelings. His father had always said he wore his emotions on his sleeve.

"I had a great time, Graham." Her gaze traveled to the road behind him, and she stiffened before she looked back. "I—I'm just not sure I'm in the right place for…whatever this is."

Her words felt like a snowball with an icy center slamming into his chest. "Right. I understand."

Was *he* even in the right place for whatever this was?

"I'll see you around at the Lodge."

He nodded and watched as she hurriedly turned to open the car door. She got inside and pulled out of the lot, ice and slush flying out behind the tires.

Her answer hadn't been a no. It hadn't been a yes either, though.

Why are women so complicated?

Graham shook his head and turned at the sound of a horn. His gaze passed over the scene but returned to a silver Range Rover parked across the street. The sight of the car tugged at something, but he wasn't sure what.

Just then, the car door opened, and a man stepped out, instantly sliding his sunglasses down from his hair.

Graham's heart stopped before thudding to life again, pulsing through his veins at the recognition of the reporter from LA. What in the world was Craig Garrett doing here? And why did it seem like Sonora had recognized him?

FOURTEEN

SONORA'S HEART pounded erratically in her ears.

"It wasn't Jonah. It wasn't him." She took a slow, deep breath as the SUV wound around the mountainous curves back toward the Lodge.

She'd seen a Range Rover that looked exactly like Jonah's, and only after he'd turned her direction had she been able to think straight. It hadn't been Jonah, but just the sight of a car like his shot worry through her. That alone had to be answer enough to Graham's request to see her again.

Then why did she want to go back and answer *yes* instead?

Her fingers flexed on the leather steering wheel. Blythe had an amazing car. It reminded her a little of the Range Rover Jonah had bought them.

Them—yeah right.

She should have known from the start it never was meant to be her car. Jonah had played it up to her, telling her all of the safety features of the expensive car and how crucial it was to buy new. He'd convinced her they needed it, and then the minute he'd driven it off the lot, she was never allowed to touch it.

She'd tried at first, thinking he would grow less attached as time went on, but he always had an excuse. Her car had better gas mileage. He had to impress his clients. She didn't know how to drive a bigger SUV. All of the reasons fell short, but she'd accepted them.

She hit the steering wheel, though not enough to cause damage. How had she missed it? And, more importantly, what was she missing with Graham?

"How about the fact you've just met him?" The words, spoken out loud, helped focus her thoughts.

She *had* just met Graham, and short of Googling him, which she was close to doing, she had one coffee date to go on. One date did not a relationship make.

Blythe's reminder sunk in. It had been just that—*one* date. Though he'd tried for a second.

The thrill his words had caused fluttered back to life, overtaking thoughts of Jonah. Graham wanted to see her again. He'd seemed eager too. And she'd all but turned him down. Or, almost.

Sonora pulled up to the gate of the Lodge, and Leo stepped out. "Howdy, Miss Sonora. You got the boss's car, huh?"

She laughed. "Yep. A little terrifying driving something so nice."

"Did you get your car all fixed up?"

"Not yet." Add that to the list of things she had to do on her off time. Yet another reason not to make more dates with Graham.

"I can have my son Lamar look at it. He works at the body shop in town, and I'm sure he'd give you a good deal."

Sonora felt tears prick her eyes, and she blinked a few times. "That would be great. If he could look at it and let me know an estimate, I could know when I'd be able to get it fixed."

"Sure thing. I'll tell him to call the Lodge and ask for you."

"Thanks, Leo. I appreciate it."

"You bet, Miss Sonora." He waved her through as the gates swung inward, and she continued on through the bare forest caked with snow.

Her emotions were all over the place, but she couldn't ignore how good it felt to have people looking out for her. It was like the time she'd spent with Donna all over again. She'd felt so alone when Jonah had all but pushed her away from their church and circle of friends. Coming to Vermont was the escape she needed, but also the beginning of a solitary life apart from knowing Blythe. Thankfully, it was proving to be anything but that.

She parked in Blythe's special spot and rushed inside the Lodge to find her friend. She needed to unpack what had just happened with Graham and all the emotions that came with it. Blythe would know what to do.

The scent of vanilla and cinnamon wafted toward her from the kitchen, and she guessed the chef was hard at work on dessert for the dinner meal that night. Her stomach grumbled in response, reminding her that coffee did not constitute a meal.

Pushing the thoughts of whatever was baking out of her mind, she moved behind the front counter when LaToya came around the corner.

"Oh, Sonora, I'm glad I caught you." The young guest services manager smiled widely. Her light brown skin offset her bright smile and glowed in the golden lights of the lobby. "There was a delivery for you."

Sonora frowned. "For me?"

"Yep." LaToya stepped past her and motioned for her to follow. "I put them back here for you."

Sonora followed the woman toward Blythe's office and gasped when LaToya pushed the door open. It was a stunning bouquet of red roses.

"Someone's got an admirer." LaToya laughed and shook her head, causing her springy curls to bounce back and forth. "I think I'm jealous."

Sonora's stomach clenched. Had Graham arranged this? It felt like something he might do, but then again, she had no idea.

You don't know him, Sonora. Not really.

"Thanks, LaToya."

LaToya winked as she stepped through the door. "Sure thing."

Sonora approached the roses, bending down to sniff. Their

rich, heady scent was intoxicating and their soft red petals velvety to the touch.

A white card popped out of a fork stuck into the middle of the flowers, and she reached for it. Her name scrawled across the front, and she couldn't help the smile. Graham had to have arranged for these to be sent. It was the only thing that made sense.

She popped the folded card open but dropped it the next second, the words seared into her memory.

Surprise.

-J

FIFTEEN

"I WANTED to punch that smug look off his face." Graham made a fist atop the white tablecloth.

"Take a deep breath, Graham." Marcus forked a piece of blackened chicken and popped it in his mouth. "He didn't see you, right?"

"Right." Graham used his fork to push around what remained of the meal. It had been excellent, but he found his appetite waning the more he thought about Craig Garrett in Middlebrook. "But he's less than fifteen minutes from here. I wouldn't be surprised if he showed up as a guest."

"No way." Marcus took a sip of water. "There is *no* way the manager would have allowed that. Remember what you told me about this week? Everyone is vetted. No press allowed."

"But he's here. Or, as close to here as he can be."

"Maybe there was a leak?" Marcus placed his cutlery across his plate and steepled his hands, elbows resting on the table. "It's the only thing that makes sense—unless someone saw you at the airport? No, that wouldn't work either. That's an hour away. How would they know where you were going?"

Graham huffed a breath and tossed his napkin next to his

plate. "I don't know. It's possible my flight plans were leaked by someone at VyCorp. That's disappointing, but an option."

"True. I can have Shelly look into it."

"Yeah, do that." Graham bit his lower lip. "What are we going to do here, though?"

"Dessert?" A waitress came up to their table, carefully piling their plates on her arm.

"No, thanks."

"Yes, please."

Both men spoke at the same time, and Marcus shot Graham a look. "*You* don't want dessert? You really are upset."

"Should I bring one to go?" The server looked between them.

"Please," Marcus said.

Graham turned his attention to the windows. It was dark outside, but white lights draped over bushes and through trees illuminated a frozen garden area that he assumed was beautiful in the spring and summer months.

"I've got an idea." Marcus grinned when Graham looked back. "Let's talk with Blythe."

"The manager?"

"Yes. We'll have Garrett put on a do not enter list or something like that. There's security here, and I don't think Mr. Garrett will hike through miles of snow to reach the resort. Do you?"

Graham pressed his lips together before shaking his head. The anger was subsiding, and as the waitress brought a boxed dessert for Marcus, Graham almost regretted not getting one for himself. The meals were all-inclusive, and he could come back and ask for something, but thoughts of perhaps finding Sonora in the kitchen again that night sounded more appealing.

Or was that a pipe dream?

He thought back to how their conversation had ended and replayed the way she'd reacted to what he could only assume was the Land Rover—or the man driving it. Was it possible she knew Craig? She said she was from Louisiana so it was doubtful, but thoughts of a past girlfriend who had only dated him for what info she could give to the press made him hesitate.

Was it possible he'd misunderstood her reaction? He thought back but was positive she'd been looking right where Craig had been. There hadn't been anyone else around, though the post office storefront was in that direction. Perhaps there had been someone else he hadn't seen.

"Come on, let's go find Blythe." Marcus stood and waited for Graham to follow. "The faster we talk with her, the faster I can dig into this dessert and call Kenna."

Graham rolled his eyes, and Marcus elbowed him in the side as they made their way from the dining room.

"How's that going, by the way? You and Kenna."

"Good." Marcus dipped his head as a smile pulled his lips upward.

"What? No sarcastic comment?"

"Things are good. Like, really good, man." Marcus shrugged. "I think this is it, you know?"

Graham stopped in the hallway. "It? As in *marriage*? You just met her."

"We've been dating for three months."

Graham sputtered a laugh. "And that means you're ready to make a life-altering decision? Three months is nothing."

"I didn't say that. At least not yet. I just have this feeling." He clutched at his chest. "Something deep. This is different."

Graham capitulated with a nod as they rounded the corner into the main lobby. His eyes roamed the room, but there was no sign of Sonora. He looked back at his friend and thought about how he'd met his girlfriend. Was it possible for something as random as their meetup to produce lasting happiness?

"I'm happy for you." Graham clapped Marcus on the back. He may not agree with how fast things were going, but Marcus was the most level-headed guy he knew. If he'd found the woman he wanted to spend his life with, Graham was all for that. "I mean it."

"I know you are. You might try to fool me, but anyone who

would dress up as Captain America for Comic-Con has to be a secret romantic."

Graham laughed. "What can I say? I've got an old soul."

They approached the desk and the young man working there. "We'd like to speak with the manager, if possible?"

"Uh, sure. Yeah." The young man pushed his glasses up and turned toward the back office before pausing to turn back. "Let me get her for you."

Blythe came out a few minutes later with the young man following her. She smiled, her gaze traveling from Marcus to Graham. A thin line creased her forehead. "Is there a problem, gentleman?"

Graham looked around, conscious of the other guests in the lobby. Most were wrapped up in conversations or a book, some even played a board game in the corner, but Marcus read his mind.

"Could we go somewhere more private?"

Her frown sharpened. "Of course. Right this way."

They walked down the hallway behind the front desk. The walls were lined with dark walnut board and batten and forest green wallpaper above it. The subtle swirling design of the paper hinted at twisting vines, and every few feet, gold sconces offset the dimness while adding elegance. Graham liked it. The whole lodge itself had a masculine feeling that appealed to him, but the softer touches—perhaps added with a woman's input—made the design feel cohesive.

"Please, have a seat." Blythe motioned to two chairs in front of a small-scale replica of the stone fireplace from the lobby before she pulled over her desk chair. "How can I help you?"

Graham looked to Marcus who was poised to take the lead, but he cut his friend off. "I was in town earlier today."

Blythe looked as if she were holding in a smile. It was clear that she knew Sonora, but just how close were they? Graham knew a little of the Lockwoods, though they were east coast old money versus his family's west coast newer wealth. It would make sense that Blythe and Sonora, both younger and who looked similar in age, might know one another. Was that why Sonora was here?

"Did something happen?" she asked.

Her question drew him from his thoughts. "Yes. Well, sort of."

"Have you heard of Craig Garrett, Ms. Lockwood?" Marcus cut in.

"Please, it's Blythe, and I have, though vaguely," Blythe said.

"He's here. In Middlebrook. I assume he's not part of your guest list, seeing as you promised there would be no one from the media in attendance this week." Marcus shifted forward, slipping easily into his role as Graham's advisor and so much more.

"No. I can assure you both that he's not on the guest list. I've gone to great lengths to keep everyone's information private, even more than my grandfather did during his tenure as manager here. We've used state-of-the-art software to ensure this. You think he's here because of you, Mr.—Graham?"

Graham could tell Blythe was nervous by the way her fingers tightened around themselves. She didn't show any other outward hints that their questions had rattled her, but he saw through her nearly perfect mask.

He couldn't blame her though. If a wealthy client like himself were to find fault with anything at the Lockwood, they could ruin not only her short career at the lodge but also the lodge's reputation.

That wasn't something he wanted to do. "It's all right, Blythe. We're not blaming you."

Her shoulders lowered a fraction.

"But we are concerned," Marcus added.

"Understandably. Do you think he's specifically here for you? He isn't…vacationing?" She looked less than hopeful.

"We don't believe so." Marcus turned to Graham. "We are in the middle of a sensitive business deal, and any type of bad press would be unfortunate."

Graham held in his smirk. Marcus had changed since they'd met as kids on the basketball court at the park near his house. Two boys from opposite sides of the income bracket but still destined to be good friends.

"All I really care about is that he doesn't have access to Lockwood Lodge. Is that possible?" Graham met Blythe's light green eyes.

"Of course. I'll inform the gate guards immediately. And I'm sorry for any inconvenience this has been for you."

"Not at all. My time here so far has been relaxing as well as enlightening." He couldn't help his smile this time.

"I'm glad to hear it." Blythe stood.

Marcus and Graham followed suit, thanking her again as they left the cozy space of her office. As he neared the door, he saw a vase of deep red roses. It was only then that he caught their fragrance as they were on a table off to the side.

His gaze darted to the card that sat on the table near them, and his heart thudded to a stop.

Sonora.

Marcus bumped into him, and Graham shuffled forward, forcing himself to take in a deep breath as he left the office. Roses like that? They had to be from someone romantically involved with her. There was no way Blythe was the gifter, or so he assumed.

"You okay?" Marcus asked.

"Yeah." Graham's throat released the word in a dry rasped. He felt Marcus's gaze on him but didn't return it. "I'm going to take a walk."

"Without your coat?" Marcus narrowed his eyes. "What's wrong?"

"Nothing." *Everything.*

"I'm going to take this decadent carrot cake to the suite. If you decide to own up to whatever is going on, you know where to find me." With a wink to soften his blunt words, Marcus left.

Graham watched him go for a moment and appreciated his friend's understanding of his moods. Marcus wasn't one to push or pry. He knew if Graham needed to talk, he would, and there was no way Marcus would push him to do that until he was ready.

Turning away from the hallway that led to the rooms on the lower floor, Graham decided to check out the library on the second floor. Maybe there was a book he could borrow since he'd finished his the night before.

Anything to take his mind off of the fact that Sonora's distance had nothing to do with him and everything to do with the fact that she appeared to be seeing someone else.

SIXTEEN

SONORA PULLED her thick cream sweater more tightly around her. She'd chosen a comfy chair on the other side of the tall Christmas tree in the lobby and hidden herself there. She'd tried to read, tried to listen to music through her earbuds, even tried some meditation on an app she'd found, but nothing distracted her from the fact that her ex-fiancé knew where she was.

But *how*?

Sonora pushed to her feet. Her teeth ground together as she turned to look out the darkened windows. It wasn't that late, but it felt later since the sun had gone down. The only light outside came from the twinkle lights wrapping the evergreen trees that lined the front drive. They glowed with pinpricks of light, making everything look inviting despite the fact it was below freezing outside.

The darkness beyond the cozy light was what bothered Sonora. A shiver raced up her spine. Was Jonah coming to bring her back to Louisiana? Or had he sent the roses as a way to remind her he was still in control?

Blythe had shared her concern and offered to take Sonora down to the police station to make a report, but Sonora knew how that would go despite the fact Blythe assured her the sheriff would take her seriously. Roses meant nothing to a man of the law. They weren't dead or black. There was no threat there. Only the threat Sonora read into them.

Was that all this was? Jonah getting into her head in his own twisted way? Sonora pushed to her feet and began pacing back and forth in front of the window. The towering Christmas tree cast off a fragrant, spicy scent that mingled with the hot apple cider at the side bar.

This was *her* Christmas. This was her escape, and she didn't want to be forced out of it based on theories. If Jonah were to show up, it was as simple as her telling him to leave, wasn't it? Or would he try to take her back?

Should she leave before he had a chance to make an appearance?

The thought stopped her in her tracks. She didn't want to leave Lockwood Lodge. She'd only been here a short time, but already it had started to feel like home. The housekeeping staff had welcomed her completely, and her cozy cottage, though small, had everything she needed.

She wasn't going to let Jonah take that away from her, too.

Spinning around, she took a step before running straight into a wall of cologne-scented muscle. "Oh!"

"Are you okay?"

Graham's hands encased her upper arms in warmth, and his eyes filled her with a strange, unexpected peace. "Graham."

"Hey. You looked pretty lost in thought. I didn't mean to interrupt your angry pacing."

She laughed, covering the sound with her hand. The lobby was mostly empty, but there were a few people enjoying the dim lighting with their books. "You didn't. Well, you *did,* but it's probably better I stop before I wear a hole in the wood floor."

"Now *that* would be some pacing." His gaze was assessing but soft. "Dare I ask what caused all of this? Did you skip dessert like I did and wish you hadn't?"

Her smile eased more of the tension gripping her muscles. "I did skip dessert, but that's not why."

"Are you sure? Because the carrot cake looked pretty amazing, and I'm still questioning why I said no to it."

"Why did you?" She folded her arms and looked up at him.

"Had some things on my mind." He stuffed a hand into the pocket of his hoodie and leaned in. "You tell me yours, and I'll tell you mine?"

A flash of embarrassment washed over her. How could she admit that she'd totally misjudged a man she'd agreed to marry and allowed him to take over her life? She looked down, the shame weighing her head.

"Hey." Graham tilted her chin up with a knuckle. "You don't have to say anything. I could go steal us dessert if that would help."

Her heart skipped a beat as the world quieted, and her focus narrowed in on Graham and his golden-brown eyes. She felt nothing but the softest touch of his knuckle and the warmth of his breath as it fanned out across her face.

What had he said? Dessert?

"Dessert is good."

His lips tilted up in a crooked smile, and he dropped his hand. "Whatever the lady wishes."

"Graham." He halted, turning back to her, but her words faltered.

"Sorry." He stepped back, and his shoulders slumped. "If you'd rather be alone, I understand. I didn't mean to interrupt your night."

He turned, and she blinked at the abrupt change. "Don't go."

He looked back. Was that suspicion she saw?

"I mean, we could settle for some hot apple cider instead. I…I don't want to be alone."

His gaze took in the Christmas tree next to them, landing on a bright red heart blown from glass. She watched his brow furrow and wondered if she'd said the wrong thing. Maybe he'd been looking for an out? But that made no sense. Why invade her space like that if he wanted to leave?

"Are you seeing someone?"

She blinked, her cheeks flushing. "What?"

"You said you weren't married, but I saw the roses in Blythe's office…"

"Roses." She licked dry lips. Why did Jonah haunt every moment of her life?

"Are you all right? You look pale." Graham rushed back to her.

She took a step back and sank into the cushioned chair.

"Sonora." Graham knelt next to her, taking her hand in his. "Are you okay?"

She hadn't wanted to have this conversation. Didn't want to tell him her pathetic past, but maybe it was the only option. The only truth she could give him.

"The roses." She bit her lip, thinking of the best way to put it but finding nothing but the truth. "They're from my ex. I think he's stalking me."

SEVENTEEN

GRAHAM'S MUSCLES TENSED. Her ex? Stalking her? That was the last thing he'd expected to hear. Perhaps a confession that she *was* seeing someone else, but not this.

"That probably came out more dramatically than I meant for it to." Sonora dropped her forehead against her palm, elbow resting on the side of the chair. She was the picture of defeat.

"Don't apologize." Graham pulled a chair closer then reclaimed his hold on her free hand, wrapping it between his own. "Can I help? Are you safe?"

She wiped at a tear that escaped, and his chest constricted. She was crying, and he wanted to do whatever it took to stop what had made her feel this way.

"Honestly…it's embarrassing," she said.

He saw the color rise in her cheeks and instantly wanted to ease her fears, but he wasn't sure what to say. Stalking was a serious crime, he knew that from the true crime podcasts he listened to, but how did a woman in her position not have personal security then?

"I left Jonah—my ex—six months ago. I found someone to stay with and thought I would be able to start again." Her voice shook, and she kept her gaze focused on the ground. "I thought I'd managed to get away, but then he found me. He wanted me to come back. Said he thought I'd made a mistake by leaving and wouldn't hear me when I said we were done."

Graham kept his voice low, gentle. "If you wanted to leave, you had every right to."

"That's what I thought. I ended up leaving where I was and came to Vermont. It was as far away as I could think to go, but then those roses showed up—"

Her voice broke, and his heart squeezed. "That must have been terrifying."

She took in a deep breath and exhaled. "It was."

"How about that cider?" He popped up, not sure what to say next. He wanted to help, but didn't know the right move.

She nodded, and he turned toward the cider bar. The scent of cinnamon and spices greeted him as he approached, but his mind raced. How could he fix this? Did she have a restraining order against the guy? Was he *in* Vermont, or had he just found out where she was? *How* had he found her?

He gripped the glass mug hard and forced himself to relax. Moving his fingers to the handle, he pulled down the spout, and warm, brownish liquid came out along with a tart apple fragrance. It made his mouth water, and he topped their drinks off with a sprinkle of cinnamon and a cinnamon stick for them both.

He placed her drink on the small table between their chairs and sat. Cradling his mug carefully between his hands, he stared into the swirling liquid.

"I wish I could do something." He said the first thing that came to mind.

"You brought me cider."

Her smile greeted him when he met her gaze. It wasn't bright or full, but he could tell she was trying. "Will he come here?"

The smile disappeared. "I don't know."

"It's okay. We'll talk to Blythe, make sure he's on a no-show list." Graham's thoughts traveled back to his own experience just an hour ago.

"I can't believe I'm in this position." Sonora's voice was thin.

Graham waited, not daring to move. He could sense Sonora was going to say something important, but he had no idea what it might be. A window into her past, perhaps? She took a sip of the hot liquid before speaking.

"It's my fault. I should have seen him for who he was—a control freak who wasn't so much interested in me as a wife but as someone he could manipulate." She looked up then, her expression softly aching. "You'd think I would have seen him coming a mile away, based on the kind of men my mom used to bring home. I swore to myself I'd never be like her—at least not when it came to dating. And what happens? I find a guy who's the same as all the men she brought home, just better at covering it up around others."

"And likely better at hiding it around you initially." Graham thought back to Monique and how she'd shown him the side of her he wanted to see. A doting girlfriend enamored with him. "But by the time you realized who he really was, it was too late, or so you thought." He searched her eyes to see if he'd come close to the truth.

She nodded. "I had plans. So many exciting things I wanted to do, but Jonah convinced me that they could wait. We dated for three years, Graham. How much time have I wasted?"

He reached out and covered her free hand with his own. "It's not a waste. I don't know you well, granted, but you don't seem like the kind of woman who sits around waiting. Maybe you weren't traveling like you wanted, but I bet you were doing things you cared about."

She nodded begrudgingly. "I helped out at my church when I wasn't working. I did what I could, but he always stopped me from doing much more than that. I had plans to travel to Namibia with our church, and he always had an excuse as to why I shouldn't go."

"Africa." Her eyes met his, and he realized he'd misjudged her. She'd spoken about travel during their date, but now he was starting to think she wanted to travel to help others, not for herself.

Sonora was amazing. What kind of man could bridle a woman like her? She clearly had a heart that wanted to help others, but he assumed some of that came with a dedication to loyalty. If this Jonah guy had convinced her he loved her and what he suggested was best for them, he could see her going along with it.

And then it was too late.

"You have nothing to be embarrassed about, Sonora." He recalled her words from earlier. "If anything, you stayed because it was the right thing to do—until it wasn't. That's brave and nothing to be ashamed of."

"I should have known." Resolve hardened her features. "But I thought I was free. Perhaps that's the worst part of all of this. He's like a bad penny, always turning up." She tried to laugh, but the sound came out hollow.

Graham released her hand and sat back in his chair. "Not here. He won't come here. All the way up in nowhere Vermont? It sounds to me like he's just trying to make a point."

"Maybe." She sipped her cider, her eyes flitting to the Christmas tree.

"Let's take a walk."

"What?" Her eyes snapped to his.

"A walk. Let's go outside and walk in the snow. Look, it started up again." He nodded toward the window where light flurries of snow drifted past.

"But you don't have a coat."

"They have loaners, I remember that from orientation. Let's do it."

"Okay." She sounded unsure, but he took it as a yes and moved to place their empty mugs in the receptacle before asking after a coat at the front desk. The young man handed over a massive, generic-looking coat with the lodge's logo on the front, and Graham turned to Sonora. She had her jacket on as well and looked out the front windows dubiously.

"Let's live a little." He grabbed her hand, though it was already wrapped in one of the gloves he'd purchased for her earlier that day, and tugged her toward the front door.

"This is crazy." She let him pull her outside.

Instead of stopping under the overhang, he pulled her all the way onto one of the winding paths that led toward the frozen garden area. The landscaping was mainly mounds of snow at this point, but the white lights sparkled, and every now and then, he'd catch sight of a red decoration or see a wreath on one of the doors to the outside. Christmas was there, but not as much as winter.

"Are you cold?" He pulled her to an alcove created by three tightly growing evergreens. Their white lights twinkled through caked on snow.

"A little." Her teeth chattered, and he turned her to face him, rubbing his hands up and down her arms to help warm her.

The action felt as natural as breathing, but his mind yanked his attention to the fact that he'd only *just* met Sonora, and his movements slowed. But instead of backing away, he took a step closer, taking his own advice to live a little.

She'd pulled the hood of her black jacket up, and white snowflakes were already beginning to congregate on the crown of her head. The guy at the front desk had given him a beanie and told him he could keep it. He'd pulled it on, but it offered little protection to the falling snow. It landed in cold points on his nose and cheeks.

"You?"

A snowflake landed on his eyelashes, and he blinked. "Me what?"

"Are you cold?" She reached up with a gloved hand and brushed a few stray flakes from his beard.

He almost leaned into the touch. Almost.

Now that they weren't moving, he knew he was cold, but there was something about Sonora's proximity that made him numb to the feeling. Or was that frostbite sinking in?

"You haven't wasted anything, Sonora." He spoke the words in a cloud of steam that rose to the heavens between them. "Don't let your ex take more from you than he already has. You've got a lot ahead of you, and I'm sure you're going to do everything you want to—and more."

She stepped closer, tilting her head back to look up at him. The hood slipped back, and snow began to land on her blonde hair. Her luminous gray eyes searched his, but his focus shifted to her lips.

The connection he felt to her drew him closer. This—whatever this was—was reckless. Feelings like this shouldn't grow so quickly, especially knowing her past was still reaching out for her. He'd known more about Monique from the start, and he'd fallen for her harder than he should have. He'd chosen to overlook things, much like Sonora said she had with her ex, and now he wondered if he was doing that with the beautiful woman in front of him.

Her guileless vulnerability stared open-faced at him, and he knew he could sink headlong into a kiss with her if he let himself. He knew he could throw caution to the wind with her, even though he didn't even know her last name.

He didn't even know her full name.

The thought yanked him out of the spell cast by her eyes, her scent, her nearness. He stepped back and threw a somewhat forced grin at her. He needed to deflect. Get some space.

"Okay, so maybe this wasn't my brightest idea. It is *freezing* out here."

She laughed, looking away. "It is. But it's also beautiful."

"Maybe we should go back. I'm afraid I'm going to lose a toe or something." He watched as she moved to the edge of the circular area, staring out into the darkness of the bare forest. The blackness stared back as he joined her.

"It's so quiet."

He looked over, and her eyes were closed. A snowflake landed on her nose, and she smiled. He moved to brush it off but caught himself before he touched her. Instead, he pulled himself out of the haze of Sonora's presence and tugged her arm.

"Let's go back before you turn into a snowwoman."

"G-g-good idea." He could see that she was shivering now.

They started back toward the lobby doors when they passed under a low-hanging branch. He didn't know where the urge came from, but he reached up and tugged it just as she walked past. A deluge of snow dropped down and cascaded all over her hood.

"Hey!" She giggled, the sound light and airy in the cold. "You did that on purpose."

"Yes I did." He kept a straight face for a half-second before he laughed.

"Not fair. I couldn't even reach that branch."

He laughed even harder as she put her hands on her hips, indignant.

Her eyes narrowed, and the devious smile that tugged at her lips brought kissing back to his mind.

Warning! Danger zone ahead.

"But don't worry. I can reach this."

She moved as if to reach another branch, but at the last second pushed him toward a big evergreen with branches coated in snow. Relying on his quick footwork from tennis, he managed to side-step face-planting in the tree, but his boot slid on ice, and suddenly, his foot was off the path. He expected to stop there, but his boot sank in deep, and the rest of him overcompensated, toppling into the snowbank at the edge of the walkway.

Dazed and instantly frozen on all sides, he looked up into Sonora's shocked expression. "I'm so sorry. I didn't think you'd fall."

She looked so earnest, and the situation was so ridiculous, Graham threw his head back and laughed. He let out the confusion of his attraction to Sonora, the questions he still had, and even some of the pent-up frustration of not being able to follow through on kissing her.

In that moment, he felt the freest he had in a long time. Libertas Retreat, indeed.

Sonora looked at him with wide, shocked eyes. "You okay? Or has the snow gone to your brain?"

"Perfect." He held out a hand, and she reached to help him up. Instead, he yanked her down next to him.

Her short scream of surprise was quickly followed by laughter. "I guess I deserved that."

"You kind of did." He sent a sideways glance at her, and they both shared a smile.

Graham knew one thing in that moment, and one thing only. If this was the time he got to spend with Sonora, then he would enjoy it and not over think it. Anything else would be too much or too little, and he didn't want to live his life like that.

EIGHTEEN

"I'VE BEEN HEARING RUMORS," Blythe said. She entered the room and moved to lean her hip against a desk in the library where Sonora had been reading after her morning shift.

"About?" Sonora closed her book, sliding a bookmark between the pages.

"Oh, I don't know. Late night walks. Coming back in covered in snow. Giggling. Things like that." Blythe's eyebrow popped in question.

"Maddox has been snooping." Sonora rolled her eyes, imagining the teen "spilling the tea" to Blythe, as he called it. "We fell in the snow. That's all."

"You know how that sounds, don't you? I mean, I'm going to need more details than that."

"It wasn't a date or anything. He just dropped some snow on me, and I happened to push him. I had *no* idea how deep the snow went, and he fell."

"And you ended up in the snow how?" Blythe crossed her arms.

"He pulled me in." She couldn't help but laugh at the memory. She'd been freezing, but there had been something peaceful about falling into the snow next to Graham.

"If that doesn't scream *romance novel,* I don't know what does."

"Come on, B. We just met. He lives in LA. I live here now." *Though he doesn't know that.* "Besides, I totally over-shared about Jonah with him, and I'm pretty sure he can tell how much of a mess I am."

"Wait. You what?"

Sonora's cheeks heated at the memory. "I mean, not everything, but he saw the roses and asked me and…it all just came out."

"Girl." Blythe pulled a chair over to face Sonora. "You hardly told *me* anything despite me practically begging for you to open up. Graham must be some kind of good listener."

"He is."

You haven't wasted anything, Sonora. His words came back to her and still gave her comfort. He'd seen through to the heart of it for her, that she'd missed out on so much by turning a blind eye to what she knew was a problem. That was the hardest part to admit to herself.

"What is happening?" Blythe shook her head. "I mean, I moved up here and was *positive* I'd never meet anyone, and here you go finding someone in the first few *days* you're here."

"Wait. What? We're not—I didn't—he's not—" She couldn't formulate her thoughts.

"You did. He is. You are." Blythe huffed a laugh. "It's too bad his friend is taken…it could have been fun to double date."

"Oh stop, B. You've got it all wrong. What makes you think I could trust someone I haven't even known for a week? I knew Jonah for years, and we know how that turned out."

Blythe's expression softened. "Don't do that. Don't blame yourself for *his* mistakes."

"Easier said than done," Sonora admitted.

"I know, but you've got to remember that not all guys will be like him." She held up her hands to forestall Sonora's retort. "I'm not saying it has to be Graham or anything, just that you should keep an open mind. You can find someone in the most unexpected of ways."

Blythe stood and walked to the door but paused. "We've got cookie decorating going on in the kitchen if you're interested. It's a lot of fun. I think Kayla was going to make a few to take home to her kids."

"Thanks. Maybe I'll check it out."

Blythe flashed her a smile before disappearing down the hallway. The room fell silent, and Sonora wondered if what her friend saw in Graham was the truth. Obviously, he was handsome and apparently, wealthy—something she shouldn't know—but was Graham as straight-forward as he appeared to be?

No one could be exactly who they appeared to be. At least, not at first and not wholly. She knew that for herself with her own background.

Shoving her book into her bag, she pushed her thoughts aside and took the back stairs toward the kitchen. Perhaps sugar and a fun art project was exactly what she needed.

The sounds of laughter greeted Sonora as she approached the kitchen. A quick peek through the window in the door showed Graham bent over a gingerbread house mid-topple. One hand held up a listing side as another attempted to squirt an unholy amount of frosting in what she assumed was an attempt to stay the collapse.

She pushed through the door and was greeted by the scent of *sweet*. Candy, frosting, gingerbread, all of it adding a festive feel to the otherwise cold-looking kitchen.

"Looks like I came just in time."

Graham looked up, his panic shifting to happiness when he recognized her, just as the other side of the house began to fall. "Oh no!"

"Let me help." She rushed to his side in time to support the other side as a girl let out a giggle across the table.

Sonora had only noticed Graham at first, but now she saw that there was a young mother with her daughter, a father with three boys, and an older couple, all creating their own houses.

"Watch out," the girl said. Her frosting-covered finger pointed to the house just as the roof began to shift.

"I think there may be something wrong with your construction here," she said. Her cheeks heated as her voice came out breathy. Graham hadn't taken his eyes off of her, and the other side of his house fell outward.

"Bah humbug." He laughed and stood up from his hunched position. "I'd hoped to create a masterpiece."

"It was looking good," the young girl said.

"Why thank you, Delilah." He dropped his head to his chest. "I'm just not as good an architect as you are."

"That's what my mom is!" The young girl beamed up at her mother.

"So what you're saying is you cheated?" Graham looked from her mother back to the girl. "I don't know if our bet can stand then."

"What bet was that?" Sonora asked. She was enjoying the banter between Graham and the girl who looked to be seven or eight. The mother watched on, though Sonora caught the appreciative way she observed Graham interact with her daughter.

"I promised to let Delilah throw three snowballs at me if she won the best gingerbread house contest." He narrowed his gaze and looked back at Delilah. "But she's a cheater."

"Am not. I did this on my own." Delilah giggled and popped her hands on her hips.

"In that case…I'd better try to salvage this. Care to assist me, Sonora?" Graham sent her a hopeful look.

"I'm not sure. Does that interfere with the rules of the bet?" Sonora looked at Delilah.

Delilah seemed to seriously consider the question. "I had my mom to help so I guess that's okay."

"Ha!" Graham pointed a finger at her, a glob of white frosting dropping onto the table with the action. "See, told you she helped."

"You know what I mean," Delilah sassed.

Delilah's mother put a hand on her daughter's shoulder. "Honey, be nice to Mr. Graham."

"I am," she insisted.

"She is." Graham backed up the statement.

"She's only eight, but sometimes she sounds like a teen," the mother said. "I'm Jessica, by the way."

"I'm Sonora." She held up her hand covered in frosting by way of explaining the lack of a handshake. Jessica just smiled.

"Okay, Sonora, we need to shore up the foundation, I think."

She looked back to Graham, who was already focused on the house. "What foundation?" She eyed the empty spot where a base should have been.

"Exactly."

He looked up at her in earnest, and she couldn't help it. She burst into laughter. "Haven't you built a gingerbread house before?"

Something—was it hurt?—flashed behind his eyes, but he smiled the next second. "Not really. Can't you tell?"

"Let's start again." Sonora leaned in conspiratorially. "I'm actually really good at this."

Delilah made a face but refocused on adding to her decorations.

They jumped back into the construction with fervor, and by the time the competition was completed, Graham had a decent gingerbread house that, while not exactly stylish, was standing.

"We did it." He held up a hand, and she high-fived him.

"Eeww. You've got frosting on your hands."

He laughed. "And you don't?"

"True."

Chef Sebastian Lee came in just then and began to pace up and down the length of the stainless steel prep table where they'd lined up their houses. He made kind comments about each one but eventually stopped at a beautiful, two-tiered house that looked almost professional.

"This is the winner," he proclaimed.

The older couple beamed at one another, and the man kissed the woman on the cheek.

"Here's a coupon for thirty-percent off in the gift shop. Thank you all for participating."

"Oh man, I didn't win," Delilah said.

Graham moved around to bend down in front of her. "Neither did I. Does that mean we tied?"

"I guess." She huffed out a breath, and Sonora fought to keep her smile in.

"How about this," Graham said. "Instead of three, you can throw one snowball at me."

"Really?" Delight shone in the young girl's eyes.

"Really." He looked up to her mom, flashing a smile. "Maybe tomorrow?"

Jessica nodded and, with a gentle hand on Delilah's shoulder, pushed her toward the door. "Thanks again, Graham. I knew she'd enjoy it if she just started."

"Of course."

Sonora watched them go and turned to Graham when they were out of earshot. "What happened there?"

"Delilah was *not* interested in doing the contest, but her mom thought that she would have fun if she just tried. I think those boys intimidated her a little." They both looked to the boys who had more frosting on their shirts than on their houses. "I decided to challenge her to the bet, and it worked."

Warmth coiled around Sonora's chest at his thoughtfulness. "That was a good idea."

"What's a little snow if I could put a smile on her face?"

Sonora nodded. "I was wondering if you'd like to—"

"There you are. You weren't answering your phone." Graham's friend Marcus rushed into the kitchen wearing a frantic look.

"What's wrong?" Graham asked.

Marcus sent Sonora a look before saying, "An urgent meeting's been called. You're needed."

Graham turned sorrowful eyes back on her. "I'm sorry. You were just going to say something."

"It sounds like you need to go. I understand." And she did. She smiled so he'd know she meant it.

"Can I take a raincheck on whatever you were thinking?"

She timidly dropped her gaze at the intensity in his expression. "Yes."

"Then I'll see you later, Sonora."

She looked up and watched him go, thinking that perhaps that had been the best outcome for the night. She'd been about to ask if he wanted to have dinner together, but now that she had space from his presence, she rethought that plan.

Graham still had no idea that she *worked* at the lodge as opposed to being a guest, and she wasn't sure what would be worse—if she told him the truth or if he found out on his own.

NINETEEN

GRAHAM GROANED as he rolled onto his back in the king-sized bed. A flick of a button sent the curtains receding to the ceiling, and he squinted against the bright morning light.

What time was it?

Shifting the clock to face him, he blinked. Nearly ten in the morning?

He sat up, the covers slipping to his waist as he fought a chill. He reached for the robe on the chair next to him and pulled it on as he slid out of the bed. The fireplace danced to life with a flick of a switch, and Graham huddled next to the extra warmth. Marcus must have turned the suite's thermostat down the night before.

It made sense. Things had gotten heated during the nearly four-hour meeting followed by the three-hour brainstorming and strategy session they'd done. It explained why he'd slept in so late, but it didn't explain the ache in his chest.

He'd missed out on…something. He'd seen it in Sonora's eyes as they made to leave the kitchen. She'd been about to ask him to do something, and then the sale he'd been anticipating had crumbled to a halt, and his presence was the only thing that could fix it.

It was fixed, or so he hoped, but it had been close. The whole thing showed him something about himself though, something he'd been trying to wrestle through and now knew the answer to.

Graham wanted to move away from the world of tech completely.

He could hear his father's disappointed words now, but he didn't care. It was his life he was living, not his father's.

Say that again and this time, believe it.

Graham rubbed a hand over his face and pushed himself into action. He'd promised to be a target for Delilah's snowball, and he had a raincheck to cash in, or so he hoped.

His stomach growled as hot water pelted his hair, neck, and shoulders. The warmth felt good, and the steam cleared up some of the grogginess, but it also gave him time to think. Sure, he could step out of the tech industry easily enough, but there were other concerns that caused him anxiety.

Selling VyCorp was the first step, but what was next? Like he'd told Sonora, he didn't know what he wanted to do. What if all his ideas focused on tech, and there wasn't anything else he was good at? Was a total career change possible? Then again, he didn't have to work.

The thought sat there staring back at him as if to challenge him. Did he really believe that? As a Hastings, there was something innate about work. It's why you got up in the morning and why you stayed up late. The accumulation of wealth was a siren's call he'd fallen prey to through the years, but there was no need for him to be a slave to it.

But what was he without work?

Then there were the thoughts of Sonora to deal with. She was a riddle to him. At one minute seemingly interested in him, and then another where she was hesitant and distant. Was he really that bad at reading women that he had no clue what she was thinking? Did it matter?

He closed his eyes and dropped his face into the stream of water. He didn't really know her, and this was a week-long vacation before Christmas. What did he expect would happen?

The story about her ex-fiancé bothered him though. The fact he'd taken the time to track her down and send her roses…it sat wrong with him. Sure, roses were an expense and not exactly creepy, but the fact that she'd left this guy, and he was clearly chasing after her was enough to make his blood boil. And that meant something.

She meant something. To him.

It's too early to know anything yet. Calm down.

The voice in his head sounded a lot like Marcus. He probably needed to run this by his best friend. Marcus had a knack for knowing when Graham was fooling himself, and his friend would have some insight into this ridiculous notion that Sonora was different than the women he usually met. Well, she was, but whether or not Graham's mind was just playing tricks on him. Or was it his heart doing that?

He shut off the water, toweled dry, and got dressed. He added another flannel to his layers and finally felt warm.

His phone rang, and he moved to the bedside table to check it. It was his father again. Someone still loyal to him had likely slipped him information about the meeting.

Graham pressed decline with only a modicum of regret and reached for his jacket as someone knocked on the door in the main area of the suite.

"Housekeeping."

His phone rang again. Still his father. He almost declined it again, but it was clear his father needed to tell him something. Perhaps the fact that he was, yet again, disappointed in his decision to sell. That he'd heard how close Rocky had been to calling the deal off, maybe?

"Hello, Father." Graham reached the door just as it opened.

"I—oh." The maid stepped back, clearly surprised he was in the room.

He turned and paced back to where he'd left his coat. "Sorry. I'll be out of your hair in a second." He needed breakfast, and he needed it fast.

"Why did you decline my other call only to answer now?"

"Morning to you, too."

"If you're going to snub me, at least commit to it."

Graham rubbed his forehead, a headache coming on. "I'm headed to breakfast. Can you make this fast?"

"Do you, uh, want me to come back?"

The maid whispered the words, and he held up a hand. He faced the windows and the freshly fallen snow, covering the mouthpiece of his phone. "Go ahead. I'll be gone in a second."

He heard the cart wheels squeak as his father replied. "Honestly, Graham, what are you doing?"

"I'm enjoying vacation for the first time in years." *Or I was until you called.* "And I'm making decisions about my life. About what *I* want to do. Why is that hard to grasp?"

"You're just like your mother."

The words hit him like a meteor impact to the chest as they'd been intended to.

"Impulsive, reckless, and selfish."

"If you want to call what I'm doing selfish, fine, but I call it self-preservation. I don't want VyCorp on my hands anymore."

"It's your legacy, boy."

"It's *your* legacy, and you bailed when things went south." *And now I'm selling it for a ridiculous profit.* He kept the words to himself, unwilling to cut as deep as his father.

"It was meant to be yours."

"I'm done arguing with you. I'm done with this conversation, and I'm done with VyCorp. And until you understand that, don't call me again." He hung up, frustration coiling inside of him like a cobra ready to pounce.

If he hadn't been so hungry, he would have gone for a run, but as it was, his anger dissipated to sadness in the span of seconds. He needed food, and he needed a distraction.

An image of Sonora came to mind. But she wasn't just distracting, she was intriguing and real. Perhaps more real than any woman he'd dated. And if she could afford a vacation at a place like Lockwood Lodge, she was in his league, too.

No worries over money. No questioning whether or not she wanted him for *him* or what he could do for her. Just two equals on the same ground with mutual respect for one another. Perhaps more than respect.

He was at the door now but paused at the sight of the woman cleaning his bathroom. Her blonde hair was pulled up into a bun.

"Is it possible to get a few extra towels? And maybe bigger ones? Those small ones are just…small." He hated how high maintenance he sounded, but he really was used to larger towels.

"Yes, sir. Of course."

He saw her shift toward him, but he was already half out the door, a hand raised in thanks. He was starving, and he needed food STAT.

TWENTY

SONORA TURNED AROUND, positive this was the moment that Graham would find out exactly who she was. Her heart pounded, and she swallowed past the dry lump of nerves and fear choking her. This was the moment she'd dreaded.

But if the truth came out, wouldn't that be better for them both?

Turning, her stomach bottomed out. The space by the door was empty. She couldn't tell if she was relieved or disappointed.

The last thing she'd been thinking of was seeing Graham when she knocked on the suite door that morning. Well, that wasn't completely true. She'd thought about how she *wanted* to see him, but her mind had been full of the job she needed to do since she'd agreed to swap Kayla's cleaning schedule for her own that day.

She should have thought—should have checked—what rooms she was cleaning. Then again, looking now, she wouldn't have recognized the last name Oswald—was that Marcus' last name perhaps? Or a fictitious one that Graham used so that Hastings wasn't recognized?

It wouldn't have mattered though. To a man like Graham, Sonora was nothing more than the hired help. He hadn't looked past her cart, nor had he looked her in the eye once. She was beneath him in every aspect, and that was clear.

Sonora bent over the sink, scrubbing the marble with extra fervor. She wasn't being fair to him, she knew that. He had been polite, if a little distant, but what did she expect? That he'd treat a maid with the same attention he did another guest? That wasn't the world a billionaire like Graham Hastings lived in.

And the conversation she'd overheard him having with his father sounded intense. Graham wasn't exactly rude, but he wasn't pleasant either. Clearly there was something going on.

A twinge of pity filtered through her focus. He had everything, or he *could* at a moment's notice, yet he couldn't buy a happy family relationship. Sonora thought of her own mother, long since passed. She'd never known her father, but at least she had mostly good memories with Mom.

She emptied the trash into the bag attached to the maid's cart and replaced it in the main sitting area of the suite. The space was stunning, like an upscale living room with a giant fireplace, over-stuffed chairs, soft throws, and a view that took her breath away. The suite was on the back side of the Lodge and faced the bare woods. Due to the nature of the land, this portion of the resort sat on a small cliff, and this room perched out just past. Looking out the window was a little like you were living in the woods in a tree-house, albeit a luxurious one.

She could only imagine how much the suite cost a night.

Stop thinking about money.

But she couldn't help the drastic difference she saw between her and Graham. He had the best of everything—clothes, shoes, rooms—and she was saving every penny just to be able to afford to pay her student loans.

She was cleaning the man's trash cans and making his bed but pretending to be what? Just another guest?

Sonora felt sick to her stomach. She couldn't keep lying to him. She had to own up to who she was.

Thoughts of what Blythe had said halted her decision. While it was fair to assume Graham had some kind of money, based on his clothes and room, she wasn't supposed to know who he really was. Did that mean she couldn't own up to him about who she was? On staff, not a guest?

Sonora aggressively pushed the vacuum cleaner across the low pile carpet. Her shoulder began to ache, and she forced herself to slow down. She was being rash. Making hasty decisions that would affect not only her new-found friendship with Graham but also her friend's position at work.

Her phone vibrated in her pocket, and as she made the last sweep of Graham's room, she pulled it out to check. It was from the pastor at the small church in town. She'd run an errand for Blythe the night before, after it was clear Graham's emergency meant he wasn't coming back, and she'd seen Jerry again. He'd told her about the pastor and the outreach program he ran, which sounded exactly like something Sonora wanted to be a part of. She'd called and left a message earlier, and now the pastor was responding.

> UNKNOWN: Hello Sonora, this is Kane Dawson, pastor of Creekside Bible Church. Thanks for your call. I'm sorry to text my reply, but we're having a Christmas play rehearsal that I need to oversee, but I wanted to get back to you sooner rather than later.

She smiled at the man's proper diction in the text and made quick work of saving his contact info.

> SONORA: Hello, Kane. I just wanted to see if there was a time I could talk to you about possibly volunteering with the outreach you run. I've spoken with Jerry a few times and he says it's a great program.

> PASTOR KANE: It is! I'll be free this afternoon if that would work? Practice should be over by 1PM.

SONORA: Perfect.

PASTOR KANE: See you then.

She pushed her phone back into her pocket, and a feeling of lightness overtook her anxiousness. She'd only been in Middlebrook a week and a half, and she was already doing more than Jonah had let her do back in Louisiana.

CHANGED and wrapped in her black down jacket, Sonora moved through the lobby toward the parking exit. Blythe had agreed to let her borrow the car again, and Sonora was excited for her meeting with the pastor.

She looked forward to getting back into volunteer work. It wasn't the same as what she'd intended to do overseas, but it was *something*.

"Sonora?"

She looked up and saw Graham. A blush flooded her cheeks at the memory of finding him at the door when she'd gone to clean his suite, and she tried and failed to tamp down the worry that he'd recognized her.

"Hi, Graham," she said.

"Would you like to go snowshoeing?"

Only then did she notice the reddish tint to his cheeks and the snowshoes he held in one hand. There were remnants of snow at his shoulder and a few stray flakes in his hair as well, and she forced herself not to reach up and brush them away.

"Delilah's work?" She motioned to the snow at his shoulder.

"She got me good." He laughed and shook his head, the longer strands that usually swept back from his forehead falling in a rakish way.

She forced herself to look away from his intense gaze. "I'm sorry, but I need to go into town."

"Are you sure? Can't that wait until later?"

"I'm afraid not." She risked a glance up and noticed he'd come closer.

"Come on, Sonora. It'll be fun. I'm sure your business can wait."

Something about the cajoling way he said it made her guard fly up. The pressing—it reminded her too much of Jonah. She would want to do something different than him, and he'd push and push until she caved.

"No." The word came out more forcefully than she'd intended.

"I—right. I'm sorry." Graham took a step back from her. "I'll see you around."

He spun away from her, and she pressed her lips so as not to call out to him. He should have taken her answer the first time. Was it a symptom of having so much wealth? He just didn't know how to handle people saying no to him?

Sonora cringed at her uncharitable thoughts. Nothing in the way Graham had acted toward her made her think he saw himself as better than her or anyone else. In fact, if how he'd acted with Delilah was any indication, he was much more relaxed than most wealthy people she'd known.

Cold air hit her in the face as she pushed the side door open, and she regretted not bringing a beanie. To her left, she caught sight of Graham snowshoeing with Marcus. He stepped forward, arms held out for balance, and almost fell over. His laugh reached her, and she forced herself to look away.

It was better this way. The more time they spent together, the more she wanted to tell him the truth, which would only endanger Blythe. Besides, there were only a few days left until the end of his retreat, and then the holiday week hit.

As far as what Blythe had told her, only a few guests were staying through Christmas. The staff would be minimal, and Sonora had offered to take as many shifts as Blythe needed her to in order to give those with families time at home.

She would be busy, and he would be gone. Just how it was supposed to be.

It wouldn't be the Christmas she'd hoped for as a young girl when she envisioned a snowy cabin, but it would be one where she was free to live her life *her* way, and that was worth the distance from friends back in Louisiana.

Sonora slid behind the wheel of the Lexus and turned on the car with a press of a button. The heated seats instantly began to warm, and she rested her head back against the buttery leather of the headrest.

This was the start of her new life. It was time for her to find her own way, not to fall prey to another guy who wanted *his* way, not hers.

TWENTY-ONE

"I THINK you've really got an eye for what we're trying to do here, Sonora." Pastor Kane Dawson was younger than she'd expected. He looked as if he was in his mid-thirties with a few gray hairs at his temple and it was clear his enthusiasm for the church and those less fortunate was his primary focus.

"I believe that, with the right tools, any organization can unleash the potential of the community to come together to help the least of these." She blushed and looked down. "Sorry, that was some of my thesis coming out there."

"Don't apologize." They walked through the modern sanctuary of the small church toward the double doors that led out into the parking lot. "I think that's a refreshing perspective. Middlebrook is small, and folks seem to think there isn't much of a difference to make."

"But there is." They stopped at the door, and she turned to look up at him. He was handsome with black hair and hazel eyes, but she only got the kindest, gentlest feeling from the man. As if he were a brother to all. That likely helped him in his position. "There are people in need here but also many overseas as well."

"I've had the dream of supporting a missionary family or

something like that as a church, but every year, we do the budget, and we're barely scraping by."

"It takes time, but I bet Creekside Bible Church can do it."

"I hope so." He smiled down at her. "Thank you for taking an interest, Sonora. I'm sorry to hear about your circumstances leading up to your move, but I hope you know you've got a church family here should you want it."

"Thank you, Kane. I do want that."

He smiled and moved to open the door for her. That's when she noticed the ring on his finger. Married then—that made sense. He was such a warm person.

"See you for the Christmas Eve service," she said. Stepping past him, she made a small wave and took the steps down to the sidewalk.

"If you need anything, don't hesitate to reach out. We may be small, but Creekside Bible Church is mighty when it comes to helping others."

"Thank you." She offered one last smile and then slid back into the comfort of the Lexus.

Her mind was swirling with ideas as she thought back on the conversation they'd shared about his hope for the local homeless and those who needed food assistance. He had programs in place, and most were running well, but he'd pointed out a few areas where he needed help. She already had a few ideas of how to streamline things, but she'd save that for another conversation. No need to bombard the man on their first meeting.

Sonora shifted the Lexus into gear and pulled out onto the main street called Middlebrook Avenue. The shops rose up to meet her, and she spotted the coffee shop where she and Graham had gone. Thoughts of warm coffee came back to her, and, on impulse, she pulled into the parking lot. Having a few moments to herself to enjoy some coffee and solitude might be good.

The scent of scones and strong coffee greeted her as she wound through the aisles of items in the gift shop. There was everything from postcards and sweatshirts to small travel necessities and full-on grocery items. It seems to be a one-stop shop and also the hub of the town if the crowd waiting for their coffee was any indication.

The line was only a few people deep so she stepped in behind a tall man and took a moment to look over the board again. She was fairly certain she wanted a peppermint mocha again, but whatever the barista had given Graham had smelled amazing as well.

The small table by the window was open, and she remembered the way their conversation had been so easy. She never would have guessed who Graham really was from that time. Perhaps a little lost, sure, but funny and—dare she think—charming.

"Miss?"

Sonora came back to her surroundings. "Sorry. Hi." It was the same young woman from when she'd been in with Graham. Penelope, as her name tag read.

"What can I get you?"

"Can I get a peppermint mocha?"

"Of course." The young woman gave her a knowing smile as if guessing customers' coffee orders was a sport to her. "That'll come right up. And what was the name for this?"

"Sonora."

"Oh, you're Blythe's friend." Penelope's smile widened. "You work at the resort, right?"

"I do."

"How do you like it? I mean, coffee is my life, but sometimes I dream about making a change."

"I'm just a maid." The realization rested heavily on her shoulders, and she was upset with herself for the shame she felt.

"Not *just* anything. Girl, that place would not run without housekeeping! Wear the job proudly." The woman's warm smile hit Sonora like an arrow to the chest that pierced through what she *thought* she should be and into the core of who she wanted to be.

She wanted to be more like Penelope.

"Thanks."

"You bet. I'm adding an extra shot to your drink - trust me, you'll thank me." And with that, she moved behind a huge machine with beans filling the top cavity. The next second, a grinder shot into gear.

Sonora moved toward the place where a dwindling line of coffee addicts waited to get their drinks. The tall man from in front of her in the line looked down and smiled.

"I couldn't help overhearing. You work at Lockwood Lodge?"

Sonora shifted awkwardly under the man's intense stare. He wore dark-rimmed glasses and had a sharp smile that added some warmth to his face but still left him looking forever-curious.

"I do." She dipped her head, pushing a strand of hair behind her ears.

Wear the job proudly.

She forced herself to look up. "I'm on the housekeeping staff."

"That's perfect."

The word felt out of place for the conversation. "Excuse me?"

"Sorry." He offered another sharp smile. "That came out wrong. Do you have a moment to talk?"

Sonora was caught off guard. She didn't get the feeling the guy was asking her to join him due to interest, but she couldn't be sure.

"I'm not really sure I have time—"

"Please. I'm a writer. A reporter actually. My name is Craig, and I'm working on a piece about the resort. I really want to get an in-depth look at it—not just the normal 'these rooms are nice' but the stuff behind the scenes. The everyday, hard-working people who make the place run."

Sonora caught herself smiling. "Really? That doesn't seem like an article many people would read."

"You'd be surprised what I can get away with." He flashed the smile again—did it always look the same?—and motioned to the table she'd shared with Graham. "So, what do you say?"

Hesitation held her back for a moment. What would Blythe think of her speaking to a reporter? Then again, the piece sounded like it would put the Lockwood in a good light. What could it hurt? She was about to say yes when a text came through.

"Sorry." She flashed a half-hearted smile at the man and checked her phone.

B: Hey girl, sorry for this but I need the car. You coming back soon?

Sonora looked back at Craig. "I'm sorry. I need to go." She sent a quick text back to Blythe saying she'd be back in fifteen minutes.

"I totally get it. What if…" He hesitated. "Don't take this the wrong way, but would you be willing to meet outside the lodge? I saw pictures of those fire pits, and they look amazing. It would just be for fifteen, maybe twenty minutes, tops."

Sonora shrugged as she reminded herself she didn't need Jonah's, or anyone else's, approval for what she did or didn't do.

"Sure, Craig. I'll meet you at the fire pits tonight."

TWENTY-TWO

"YOU OKAY, MAN?" Marcus came out of his room wearing sweatpants and no shirt. His hair was wet, and as he moved toward the fire like a moth to a flame, he pulled his long-sleeved shirt down over his shoulders. "You've been off today."

Graham looked up from the book he'd borrowed from the library. It wasn't as good as the space opera he'd finished, but it was doing its job distracting him from real life.

"I'm fine."

Marcus stared at him.

Graham knew he wouldn't push, but he wasn't sure what he wanted. Did he want to talk to his best friend about Sonora's brush off? Or did he want to sink back into a world of water and evil queens?

"It's Sonora."

Marcus didn't say anything. Instead, he slid into the oversized chair that looked more like a loveseat and pulled a blanket over his legs.

"I tried to get her to go snowshoeing with us earlier today."

"I saw you talking with her," he said by way of acknowledgment.

"I think I pressed too hard."

"No. You?" Marcus' words bled with sarcasm.

"You know how I get when I want something. I don't let up. I just can't stop thinking about it."

"Her refusal or your pushing?"

Graham frowned. "What do you mean?"

"Are you more concerned with the fact she snubbed you, or that you pushed too hard?"

He dropped the book onto the side table, all thoughts of reading vanished. "I don't know."

"I'd just say that the answer to that question will say a lot about you."

"In what way?"

"If you're more bothered by the fact she turned you down than you are the fact you might have pushed her too hard, then I'd say *you're* the problem."

Marcus had a great, albeit painful, way of getting to the heart of matters.

"What if it's both?"

"*Buzzz.*" He made a sound that was reminiscent of a buzzer from a game show. "Wrong answer."

"Are you saying I'm being selfish?"

"Not in so many words." Marcus grinned at the eye daggers Graham shot him. "I'm just saying that you tend to get bull-headed about your way. I think your past girlfriends might have overlooked that as a way to stay in your good graces, but if Sonora isn't okay with it, then that's telling."

"How so?"

"It means she's not going to put up with you getting what you want."

Ouch. "Please, tell me more about how awful I am."

"Stop it." Marcus launched one of the throw pillows at Graham, narrowly missing the cup of water he had on the side table. "I'm not letting you get off that easy."

"Fine. I concede you *may* have a point."

Marcus raised his hands up. "Goal! Score one for Marcus."

Graham rolled his eyes. "What do I do about it? That's the more important question."

"What you should do every time you plow over someone else's desires. Apologize."

"I know that."

Marcus frowned. "I'm confused. What are you asking me then?"

"I'm saying…what do I do *after* I apologize?"

"Ask her on another date?" Marcus shrugged. "Graham, we only have a few days left. Either decide that this is something or it's not, but make a choice. I can track her down once we're back to L.A., but I'd really rather you man up and ask her for her number before it comes to that."

Graham laughed, shaking his head. "So you think it's—*she's*—a good idea?"

"I don't know, but I haven't seen you like this about a woman in a long time. Yeah, you liked Monique, but dare I point out most of what you liked about her was her poise and good looks."

Graham grimaced. "She was nice to talk to."

"Was she, though?" Marcus looked skeptical. "I feel like most of the conversations I was around for dealt with you talking about some new thing you wanted to do and her being on board. Every time."

Graham couldn't argue. Monique had been *very* agreeable, but seeing how things ended for them, he shouldn't be surprised.

"I guess Sonora is different."

"She is. So you just give me the word, and I'll background check her and—

"Marcus."

"What? It's my job."

"I thought you told me to man up and ask her for her number?"

"I did, but that doesn't mean I still won't look out for you. I don't care if she's old money, a CEO of Microsoft, or she won the lottery—I'll need to know more about her should anything progress. You can be you and leave all that to me."

Graham slapped his hands on his knees and shoved to standing. "Fine. You be you. I'll be me. Wish me luck."

"What are you doing?"

"Going to see if I can get her number."

Graham pushed the door out into the hallway and noticed his hands were shaking. Was he nervous? He paused in the hall as the door clicked shut and took a moment.

He *was* nervous.

He'd squared off with CEOs of Fortune 500 companies. He'd made presentations to thousands. But the thought of seeing Sonora made him nervous? What was that about?

Marcus' insight was likely part of the reason. Graham appreciated his friend's perspective and knew he was right, but he wasn't sure exactly how to tell Sonora that. Just apologize? Or press to see if she felt even a little of what he was? He didn't want the week-long retreat to end without saying something to her.

But what could he say aside from the fact that he wanted to see her again? Was that enough? Since they were both at this retreat, it made sense to think that they each had the means to make that happen, but what could that lead to? Anything? Or something?

Graham ran a hand over his beard. Deep down, he wanted to have what he hadn't as a kid. A family. Real and loving. If he kept dating women like Monique, he knew that wasn't going to be possible. Or perhaps it wasn't *impossible,* but it wasn't going to be what he wanted. Any woman who would date, and perhaps marry, him for money wasn't the kind of woman who would stick around when things got tough. At least not if his mother was any indication.

Graham forced his feet to move down the hall in search of Sonora. He'd never been the kind of guy to lay it all out, but maybe that was what this situation warranted. As crazy as it sounded that he could meet someone like her and think of forever in the span of days…there was something there. At least for him.

He'd be a fool not to ask her if she felt even a portion of that too.

Graham pulled his shoulders back, thrust his chin out, and stepped into the lobby area. It was nearing time for dinner and already dark outside, but the warm glow of the lobby Christmas trees and the soft sound of instrumental Christmas music filled him with sudden hope.

It was the season for miracles, wasn't it?

He diverted toward the front desk but slowed down when he saw a familiar head of long, blonde hair.

"Sonora," he called out just as she stepped outside, hands holding two cups of steaming liquid.

He rushed around the desk and dodged a couple walking toward the dining room. Now that other guests had arrived at the lodge, it was hard to tell who was who, but Blythe had assured their group that no one would know who they were or anything about the retreat.

So far, she'd done a great job of keeping things on the down low. He'd heard tales of the retreats years prior when Blythe's grandfather had coordinated them. They were more lavish, but in her introduction email, Blythe had explained why she'd taken a more relaxed approach. If they truly wanted to escape their normal lives, the best way to do that was to relax, enjoy the scenery and events the lodge had to offer, but not to feel like they were still at home on their estates or lavish homes.

Blythe's email had spoken to Graham in a way he hadn't expected. He did get bored of the everyday attention of the help he hired and the lavish life he lived. It sounded arrogant, definitely something Marcus would laugh at him for thinking, but it was true. And Blythe spoke as someone who knew what that was like and had found a better way.

Graham reached the glass door to the outside but paused.

Sonora was sitting at one of the fire pits, a blanket draped over her legs and her hands extended to the heat, but she wasn't alone.

At first, Graham thought the man might be her fiancé, but she was smiling and didn't appear to be afraid or forced to be there. His worry tamped down some, but then the man she was speaking with shifted at the same moment a flame flared up, illuminating his face.

Graham froze in place, his mind not able to comprehend what his eyes were seeing.

It was Craig Garrett, and it looked like he was interviewing Sonora.

TWENTY-THREE

SOMETHING WAS WRONG. Sonora hadn't sensed it at first when she'd met Craig at the fire pits. At first, he'd asked her about her job and jotted a few notes down, but then something shifted. That's when she'd started to wonder what he was really doing there.

That's when she'd excused herself to get them tea from the kitchen. She'd needed a moment to think—to ask herself if she was just hesitant with all men because of Jonah, or if there was truly something wrong.

Now, as she took a moment to sip the cinnamon tea, she took stock of how her body was reacting. Her chest was tight, abdomen slightly queasy, and her shoulders stiff. The reaction had happened the moment Craig mentioned Graham by first *and last* name.

"Would you say that Mr. Hastings is under any kind of stress this week? I mean, I've heard things about the retreat, but he doesn't strike me as the kind of guy who would know how to relax well."

"You know Graham?" Her brow furrowed. No one should know about the retreat, and no one should know Graham was there. At least, that's how she'd understood Blythe's explanation.

"Doesn't everyone?" Craig laughed, but the humor never reached his eyes. "We go way back."

Somehow that sounded like a threat, not a true connection.

"What did you say this article was about again? The Lodge?"

"Yeah. And those that vacation here. You know, the upper crust. People that are nothing like us."

Her eyes narrowed and took in the reporter's expensive gold watch, high-quality leather shoes, and brand name jacket. He was playing down to her, and she could see the signs clearly now. The ones that pointed to her being taken in by his charm. She'd done it again.

"You know what, Mr. Garrett, I think—"

"What in the world do you think you're doing?"

She started, hot tea splashing her hand. "Ouch."

"Well, hello, Mr. Hastings." Craig grinned up at Graham who stood over him, a scowl marring his handsome features.

"Sonora, why are you talking with him?" He turned to look at her, and some of the anger faded to hurt. "He's..." he shook his head as if he couldn't think of the right word.

"I'm a dog with a bone, Mr. Hastings. And that means I *always* get my story."

"What story?" Sonora asked. She sensed there was more here than what she'd initially thought, but it also acted as confirmation that what she'd sensed was true. Craig was up to no good.

"What did you tell him, Sonora?" The hurt on Graham's face sharpened to worry.

"Tell—what?" She looked between them again.

"I think I can have the story ready to go by the morning. What about the headline 'Billionaire flees as VyCorp sale marks the end of his career?' Has a nice ring to it, doesn't it?"

"Sonora," Graham said her name like a curse. "How could you?"

"I didn't do anything." She shot to her feet, tea forgotten on the side table. "And I hope that you'd have more sense than to think I'd go behind your back and say *anything* about you."

She turned to go and heard Craig laugh. "She's not your normal type, Hastings."

She froze, feet rooted to the ground.

"She's not your concern, Garrett, and you'd better get off this property before I have security throw you out."

Sonora breathed again. Even though she was mad at Graham for not believing the best of her, she was also still worried about the truth coming out. Or perhaps it was more *how* the truth came out that she cared about.

"How about a comment I can print, Mr. Hastings?" Craig's voice was a sneer.

"No comment."

"Not even about this new potential woman in your life? That will add some juicy tidbits. I mean, she's just a—"

Sonora rounded on them both, though they were now several feet away. She wasn't going to let this creep tell Graham the truth she should have already spilled. "Graham—"

"It's time for you to leave." Marcus rushed past her with two resort security guards in tow.

"Brought in the calvary from the other side of the tracks, huh?" Nothing seemed to phase Craig as the guards each took an arm and began to escort him from the property.

"Thanks for letting me interview you, Sonora," he called out. "It's going to make for a very interesting article."

She pressed her fingers to her forehead. Nothing about this night had gone as planned. Why hadn't she listened to her gut instantly when something felt off with Craig?

Turning to go, Graham called out after her. "Sonora, what did you say? What did he mean?"

"I told you. I didn't say anything." She cast a glance behind her, but she couldn't tell what he was thinking from his stony expression.

Marcus looked between them, and when she met his gaze, it was narrowed. A protective, assessing kind of gaze.

Sonora turned away from them both and headed inside. She

either had to tell Graham the truth or make it clear she wasn't interested. This back and forth, trying to figure out the man's thoughts and her own feelings was getting even more confusing—if that were possible.

Warmth greeted her along with the tantalizing scents of dinner and the cider on the other side of the lobby, but she wanted none of it.

"There you are." Blythe rushed up to her and latched gently onto her arm. "Come with me."

Confused, Sonora let her friend lead her back to her office. Blythe closed the door and then turned to her.

"Did you tell that reporter anything?"

"Are you joking?" Sonora's ire rose. "Why does everyone assume I said anything at all?"

Blythe was stunned by Sonora's outburst.

"Sorry," Sonora said. "I just left Graham looking at me like I'd betrayed him *and* Jesus or something."

"What?" Blythe shook her head. "Sorry, never mind. And I don't mean to insinuate you'd say anything. I just needed to know if you did say something. Not because I don't trust you, but because I have to get out in front of this."

"This?" Sonora sunk down into the cushioned chair and wished the fireplace was turned on. She was cold from being outside but perhaps cooler after the look of betrayal Graham had sent her way.

Blythe sat on the chair opposite her. "Leo came rushing up here from the guard post saying that Adam was watching the service gate and let some guy go through. He got two hundred dollars for it and wanted to split it with him if Leo wouldn't tell. Leo's a valuable employee and still employed, which is not what I can say about Adam."

"That's how Craig got in?"

Blythe's eye twitched. "You're on a first name basis with him?"

"No. It's not like that." Sonora pressed her fingers to the bridge of her nose. "I met him in Middlebrook this afternoon, right before you texted, and he asked to interview me for an article since I was a maid here."

"How did he know?"

"Penelope at The Grind mentioned something about it, and he must have overheard."

"Right." Blythe urged her on with a nod.

"I told him I couldn't stay to talk, but he suggested meeting at the Lodge."

"So he knew even then he could get in? I wonder if he's been up here before. I should have asked Adam that before I fired him." Blythe let her head roll back while she let out a sigh. "This could be really bad."

"I guess I don't get it. I mean, I didn't tell him anything he didn't already know, and when he started asking about Graham, I knew something was wrong. I clammed up and was going to leave when Graham found me."

"That must have been right before I called Marcus and told him Craig was on the property."

Sonora nodded. "Yeah, Marcus showed up with security to take him away. I—I still don't understand though."

"I don't completely either, but I do know that Graham is in the midst of some big deal, and from what Marcus said, Craig's been out to nail Graham for a long time. Not sure if there's some history there we don't understand, but he's trying to get dirt on him. I'm just afraid he found out about the Libertas Retreat in the process."

"He didn't find out from me, but I think he already knew something about it." Blythe's eyes widened, and Sonora rushed to reassure her. "I'm sorry, B. I never would have even spoken to him had I known, but he didn't know details. Just that there was a retreat. I doubt he knows what it's really about."

"I suppose it was bound to get out someday, but I manage the guest list so carefully. Even the guests who aren't part of the retreat are vetted. No one should have said anything."

"They wouldn't. I know you, B. you've got a handle on this,

and everything will work out." Sonora wanted so badly to talk to her friend about Graham, but in that moment, she saw the heavy burden Blythe was carrying.

"I hope so." Blythe slumped back against her chair.

It wasn't fair to tack on her worries. "You know what?" Sonora leaned forward. "Let's put those fancy lawyers to work."

"Lawyers? What?"

Sonora grinned. "You always used to say your grandfather had all these lawyers on retainer when we were in college. Remember?"

"You mean when I would say I wanted to use them to get out of taking a test?"

"Yes!" Sonora joined her friend in smiling at the memories. "I assume they weren't just figments of your imagination. There has to be some type of legal angle we can use to silence Craig's article if he's actually writing something."

Blythe's manicured nail tapped against the arm of the chair. "You know, you may have something there. What if I were to call his editor? Surely there is something the Lockwood name can do to get them to stop a possibly slanderous article."

"And you're sure that's what he's doing?" Sonora knew the man wasn't reputable, at least not in the way he'd gone about getting onto the property and the reason why he wanted to speak with her, but it was still surprising to know he was acting even more underhandedly."

"We can't be sure, but we can make a call." The hope that flashed in Blythe's eyes renewed Sonora's hope as well.

"Let's do it."

TWENTY-FOUR

"WHAT WAS THAT ALL ABOUT?" Marcus stared Graham down, firelight flickering against his set features. "Sonora was talking with Craig?"

"No. Well, yes, but she says she didn't share anything."

"And you trust her?"

Indignation puffed out Graham's chest. "Yes." *Don't I?*

"Do you? I mean, I don't know how much damage control I need to do."

"I...I don't know. I mean, she *said* she didn't say anything, and I believe her, but it was shocking, to say the least, to see her speaking with that scum bag."

"I'll bet. Just as shocking as when Blythe told me what happened."

"What did happen?" Graham shifted closer to the fire.

"You want to go inside?"

Graham took in a deep breath and looked up at the stars above them. The outdoor lights had gone off once the security guards had taken Craig away, and now only the firelight illuminated the space. It made room for a blanket of stars shining like pinpricks of ancient light acting to remind Graham just how small he really was.

"Let's sit for a bit."

Marcus shrugged and moved to place another log on the fire. It popped and crackled as the dry bark met flame, and the light brightened for an instant. Graham picked the chair Sonora had vacated and pulled the blanket she'd used over his lap.

He wished she were here talking with him instead of Marcus, but he'd botched that when he'd gotten angry at her and accused her of consorting with the likes of Craig Garrett. Then again, Craig had said she'd given him something to use.

"Can you tell me what happened?" Graham said, pulling his thoughts from what Sonora may or may not have said.

Marcus ran through a crazy story of how Craig had bought his way onto the property and how that gate guard was now looking for another job.

"I feel a little guilty. There can't be that many places for employment around here."

"It's not your fault that guy took a bribe and lost his job." Marcus stared into the flames. "What I don't get is how he even knew you were coming here in the first place."

"I hate to say it but…Monique?"

Marcus snorted. "You think she did it to get back at you for dumping her?"

"She knew about the retreat, but I didn't share many details with her per the NDA. I'd even considered bringing her." He dropped his head into his hands. That would have been disastrous.

"Glad you didn't." Marcus made a face.

"Why didn't you tell me how you felt about her?"

"It's your life to live. Believe me, if you'd said you were going to propose, we'd have had words, but I didn't feel like it was the right time to bring up any of my concerns."

"Concerns. As in *multiple* concerns?"

"We've been over this. I'm just glad you saw the light." Marcus' phone buzzed, and he pulled it out of his pocket. The smile his phone illuminated told Graham all he needed to know.

"Kenna?"

"Yeah. Sorry." He sent another text and shoved the phone into his pocket.

"If you need to chat with her, that's totally fine."

"This is more important." Marcus leaned forward, elbows on his knees. "Sonora."

He only said her name, but Graham knew what he was getting at.

"She didn't share anything." He said the words again, but this time, he believed them.

"Okay, then my next question is simple: what are you going to do?"

"You mean in the next two days before we fly back to L.A.?" Graham looked up to the heavens again as if the stars held the answer.

"I mean in general. There's something there between you—and don't tell me I'm seeing what I want to because I'm happy with Kenna. It's not that at all."

"We need to talk, that's clear, but I don't know. I think I'm on the cusp of something here."

"How so?"

"With all that's going on with VyCorp and the sale, I've gotten used to thinking of myself as a free man, but I haven't given any thought to what that freedom will be used for."

Then again, he couldn't really say that was fully true. There had been something in the way Sonora had talked about traveling and helping others that had sparked something inside of him. He was wary of that impulse though. The one that pushed him to try something new when what he should really focus on was making himself the *real* version. Not anyone else's wishes about who he could or shouldn't be. Not his father. Not his executives at the company. Not even the media who portrayed him as a billionaire with a squirrel's attention span when it came to dating.

"You've got a lot of space ahead of you. I don't think you need to fill it with the first thing that comes around." Marcus leveled a look at him. "I know you want to find the next thing and dive headfirst into it, but I'm just saying take a bit to settle into life without the corporate shackles."

Graham felt an eyebrow raise. "Shackles, huh?"

"I've stayed with you at VyCorp because I believe in *you*, not because I'm passionate about what we do. Not really. I honestly think that whatever you do decide to do next, you're going to be great at it, and I want to help you with that, but I'm not going to push you into it."

"Even if that puts you out of a job?"

"We all benefit from the sale, you know that. I'll be all right."

Graham frowned. "You'd tell me if you need anything, right? Like, anything?"

"My own private jet could be nice," Marcus said. He leaned back, looking into the sky as if he were imagining it now.

"Let me make a call." Graham pretended to reach for his phone before they both broke into laughter. "Okay, so maybe not *anything*."

Marcus sobered. "I know what you mean, and I'm here for you too. I may not be able to give you anything substantial, but I'll always be a sounding board, and I'll give you advice. And my advice is to run after Sonora. Don't walk, don't pass go—run. She's something real in your life that has affected you, and I haven't seen that in a long time."

Graham considered his friend's words and knew they rang with truth. Marcus knew him better than anyone, and he trusted him exclusively with his life. If he was saying he saw something in how Sonora had affected Graham, that meant something.

"We just met though," Graham said. His hesitation had nothing to do with the woman, and everything to do with his own background and track record. "What if I mess this up?"

"I think the fact you're asking that question is a good thing. And want to know my last piece of advice?"

"You know I do."

"Don't mess it up."

TWENTY-FIVE

SONORA COULDN'T BELIEVE she'd gone almost the whole day without seeing Graham. After the incident the night before and the hours she'd spent with Blythe calling first one lawyer and then another before finally getting through to someone who understood their predicament. And then the call to the editor. That had gotten to a level of heated Sonora had never experienced in a professional setting.

Her shoulders slumped just thinking about the conversation again as she pulled on her knee-high brown boots and wrapped a cream knitted scarf around her neck. The editor had insisted they had no legal claim, and the worst part was that Blythe's lawyer had agreed.

Blythe had been inconsolable, but Sonora continued to remind her that they had no idea what Craig was going to say. While she hadn't shared this thought with Blythe, Sonora felt as if Craig was more interested in nailing Graham for something. She still wasn't sure what though.

She stepped outside into the frigid air and took a moment to enjoy the scene before her. The path that led to the side entrance of the Lodge was slowly turning white where the thick snowflakes fell.

Everywhere else the snow joined the already formed piles, and she couldn't help but remember falling into the one with Graham. Her cheeks heated despite the cold surrounding her, and she admitted to herself that she wanted to see him. Wanted to talk things out.

Sonora started down the path, mindful of her steps on the slick snow, knowing that the tread on her boots had worn down years ago. It was like walking through a wonderland, and the silence that descended around her was comforting in a way she hadn't anticipated. This was her new life. Her new state. And slowly, she was growing accustomed to it in a way she'd never expected.

The snow wasn't a bother so much as it was a fixture. The work wasn't hard but fulfilling. And the people she'd met on staff she could already count as friends. Leo's son Lamar had quoted her a very reasonable price to fix her car, and she'd been invited to a New Year's party by Kayla.

Things were falling into place. A little like the snow that blanketed the grounds of the Lockwood Lodge.

The faintest sound of Christmas music came to her as the outdoor speakers came into range. If she had to spend Christmas alone, this was the place to do it. Blythe would be flying to New York, and LaToya would take over as manager for the week. But even though Blythe had invited her to join, Sonora had declined.

It felt right to be here. Right to celebrate new beginnings and a new start here in Vermont.

The warmth of the hall flooded into her, and she unwrapped one layer of her scarf now covered in a light dusting of snow. She stamped her boots, getting most of the snow off, and then set off down the hall. She wasn't too hungry after taking part in the lunch buffet and salad bar set out every Thursday, but she was in the mood for some hot cocoa and reading.

The scent of chocolate greeted her like a long-lost friend as she moved to the hot cocoa bar area. The various toppings awaited her in their pristine glass jars with the airpots all lined up and waiting.

The sight put a smile on her face, but it dimmed when she saw the maple syrup, and her thoughts strayed to Graham.

She knew what room he was in, but she couldn't just show up there. He wouldn't believe that anyone would give her that information at the front desk, and she didn't want to lie anymore to him. Perhaps if she sat in the lobby he would come by, and she could catch him for a talk. She owed him an explanation about Craig, even though there wasn't anything to explain. Not really.

She opted for white chocolate chips at the bottom of her mug, a generous pour of dark chocolate, and a dash of peppermint. Adding a candy cane again, she used it to stir the white chocolate chips until they melted as she moved toward a chair in the corner.

The first sip was bliss, and she carefully placed her cup on the side table to pull out her paperback from the pocket of her jacket. It was a small, cheap fantasy her mother had read so many times the cover was almost falling off, but Sonora read it every year around Christmas time since it was the story of a winter princess and a race to find her prince before the New Year.

Sonora felt a little like that princess, but instead of wanting to find someone else, she wanted to find *herself* before the New Year. She took another sip and let her gaze stray to the white snow. It was fresh and clean, and she wanted that for the New Year. For her new life.

It was one thing to *want* to find yourself and another to trust who you were becoming. She wasn't sure she could do that yet.

"Sonora."

The voice speaking her name wasn't the one she'd expected. "Marcus. Hi."

He flashed a smile as he moved toward the hot cocoa bar. "I've got an insatiable sweet tooth, and this hot cocoa bar is probably the worst—and best—thing that could be here 24/7."

She laughed. "I can admit I've indulged more than I probably should have too."

Marcus took his time adding toppings to his mug before he turned and faced her, his eyes narrowing. "About last night."

She wasn't sure why she'd known he had a purpose for being here, but the minute he'd appeared, she'd just known. And she also knew it had to be about Graham. She chose silence, letting him proceed as he wanted.

"I think it would be best to fill you in on just who Craig Garrett is. To Graham, that is." Marcus took a seat, his hands cupping his hot cocoa. "About ten years ago when Graham's father gave him control of his company, Craig caught wind of it. I guess there's some type of history between Craig's father—who also works in the tech industry—and Graham's father. A lot of bad blood, and Craig saw this as his opportunity to smear Graham's name and reputation across the news as best as he could."

Sonora couldn't imagine what it was like to be in the public eye like Graham was.

"He did a deep dive into Graham's past and found some… difficult things. Not because Graham did anything." Marcus rushed to assure her. "Just that Graham's past is, well it's *his* story to tell so I won't get into that, but Craig dug it all up and was going to print."

"But he didn't, did he?" Sonora's fingers clenched her mug so tightly the hot liquid threatened to burn her.

"His editor was paid off by Graham's father, and I don't think Craig's ever gotten over it. Ever since, he's been gunning for Graham. It's funny though—there's nothing to uncover. I mean, I'm not just saying that because I'm his friend and I work for him. It's actually true. He's a good guy who trusts too easily, I think."

A chill raced up Sonora's spine at the clouded look in Marcus's gaze. "And what about you? How did you two get to be such good friends?" She hoped her change in topic might shift the pressing nature of Marcus' stare.

He paused to take a sip. "We were two boys from opposite sides of town that shouldn't have been friends. I know, sounds like a bad beginning to a movie. We ended up at the same basketball court one day and started playing. He was terrible." Marcus laughed, clearly going back in time with his thoughts. "I decided to help him, which meant totally annihilating him in the game."

It was Sonora's turn to laugh. "You didn't."

"Oh, I totally did. And he needed it. We became good friends after that." Marcus' brow furrowed. "Even when his father didn't want him hanging out with me, he stood up for me and our friendship. He's been with me through it all, and I owe him…well, my life. But that's another story."

"I know how that goes." Sonora dropped her gaze to the dregs of her cocoa, dark chocolate and half a mini marshmallow lingering at the bottom of her cup. She knew friendship like that. Blythe had been there for her no matter what, especially now.

"Sonora." Marcus said her name with added weight. "Graham is my best friend. He's practically my brother. Aside from it being part of my job, *literally,* to look out for his interests, I also do that because I care about him."

"Those types of friends are important." Her mouth went dust-dry, and she wished she still had cocoa to soothe it.

"They are. You and Blythe have that kind of friendship, don't you?"

His words hit the mark they were intended to. "We do."

"I don't want Graham to get hurt. If there's something going on." He leaned back in his chair, and she saw the truth of it. He thought she was in on some type of scheme.

"You don't think I am connected to Craig in any way, do you?"

"I don't know what's true."

There it was again. The stab of truth. He'd done his research on her, and he knew. Knew she wasn't on Graham's level by a long shot. But had he told Graham then?

"I wouldn't do that—to anyone." *Let alone Graham.* "But just as you said Graham's past is complicated, so is mine." She bit her lip. Should she tell him the whole truth?

But he stood, his mug now empty. "I can understand that, but I also need to look out for my friend. Can you assure me that your intentions are honorable toward him?"

It felt backwards, like the kind of talk a father should have with their daughter's boyfriend, and Sonora wanted to laugh despite the fact she found no actual humor in the encounter. But looking at Marcus now, she could see what he was doing. He was testing her but also staying true to his affiliation to Graham. If it was true that he did know who she was—*what she was*—and he was letting her keep her secret for now, he must see a reason for it.

She met his gaze, and the truth clicked into place with the single word she uttered. "Completely."

"Then I suggest you tell him that." Marcus shrugged and offered her a half-grin. "And maybe the rest of the truth. He's a good listener."

TWENTY-SIX

THE FIRE SPIT sparks into the air as a pocket of pitch superheated from the embers. The scent of woodsmoke and pine wafted toward Graham, and he took a second to close his eyes and take in the moment.

It was so cold he almost couldn't feel his nose, but the chill was refreshing somehow. Needed after a long day stewing inside. The warmth from his spiced apple cider heated his hands as the flames sent warmth toward him, but behind him, everything was cold and dark.

They'd done everything they could, but the article was running tomorrow. A leaked early copy had greeted him from his email inbox, and despite himself, Graham had read it. It was unflattering, as he'd expect anything from Craig would be, but at the end of it all, Graham saw the piece for what it was. A man preaching wild accusations to assuage his anger over something Graham never had a hand in.

The fallout might swell and bluster for a few weeks, but he doubted it would have much weight once the New Year hit. Or maybe that was his wishful thinking.

Did it matter if Craig Garrett painted him as a comfort-seeking, impulsive man who left broken hearts in his wake? Not really. Though the quote from Monique had been a sharp dig to his ribs.

"He's like any other rich guy—out for himself."

Was he like that? He'd tried so hard *not* to be that guy, but here he was, escaping a business he'd committed to. The sale that, from his perspective, would be best for his employees, but from the outside looked like he was just another bored, rich kid seeking a new adventure.

Graham had been assured that the current employees would be taken care of. He'd had it written into the contract that no layoffs would happen for the first year so that, should anyone want to leave, they could, but they wouldn't be forced to. The employees would also be getting a generous check due to the sale.

But here he sat in Vermont, on the night before the big company Christmas party, thinking about himself.

He should be at the party. He should have done a lot of things.

His thoughts trailed to Sonora and how he'd accused her of being in league with Craig. It was an absurd notion, but it *had* come to mind. He was just like his father in that way, thinking that there might be ulterior motives behind those he drew close to.

Graham took a sip of his rapidly cooling cider and let his gaze bore into the embers. He wanted more out of life, but was it possible he was just looking for some type of personal fulfillment?

When Sonora talked about the things she was passionate about, they didn't center on how those things made her feel. It was all about those she could help.

He let his head fall back against the Adirondack chair, eyes reaching to the stars as if the answers to his questions rested there. Perhaps they did. Any answer he sought within himself only turned up empty.

"Hi."

He jerked forward, some of his now-cool cider spilling over to his hand. "Sonora."

She stood on the other side of the fire, a thick red scarf

wrapped around her neck. She wore her puffy black jacket, jeans, and fur-lined boots. She looked amazing.

"Hi."

"Can I join you?"

"Of course." He sat up straighter and put his abandoned cider on a small table next to him, the tangy-tart sweetness of it gone from his mind. "Are you cold?"

"I'm fine." She perched on the edge of a chair across from him, her knees nearing the fire pit.

"You look cold."

She dipped her head, her nose disappearing into her scarf. "Maybe a little."

"Here." He stood and pulled out a thick wool blanket from the lidded container next to the extra stack of wood and moved to her side of the fire, bending to drape it over her shoulders. "Better?"

"Yes."

He took the opportunity to take the seat next to her, angling so he could face her. "I'm sorry about last night." He'd wanted to apologize all day but hadn't been able to find her.

"I'm sorry too."

"You have nothing to apologize for."

"But I do." The grave tone of her voice drew him up short.

"What—"

"Let me explain." Her eyes met his, asking for his cooperation.

"Okay." He nodded and pressed his lips together to ensure he didn't interrupt her.

"I haven't been completely honest with you."

Her words landed like hot coals in his stomach, but still he kept his lips pressed tight.

"I didn't lie, not exactly, but I think I let you believe what you would about me, and despite what you may think after I tell you this, I wanted to put it all out in the open first."

She dropped her gaze, and he wanted to reach out and tilt her chin up, but he held his hands fisted in his lap.

"I'm not an attendee at the Libertas Retreat. I'm actually not even a guest." She swallowed. "I'm just a maid."

The words landed between them, and he fought to understand. A…maid? Like housekeeping?

"I'm sorry that I let it go on this long with you thinking I'm someone I'm not." Sonora sent him a fleeting look. "I didn't know what to do when Blythe accidentally told me who you are."

The coals turned to ice. She knew who he was? Had she been playing him this whole time? Pretending to have money when in reality, they were worlds apart? A sickening feeling washed over him. Was it more than that? Had she…targeted him? Maybe he hadn't been that far off after finding her with Craig.

"You've got to be kidding me." He shoved to his feet.

"Graham, please—"

"For just *once*, I wanted to find someone I could see eye to eye with. I'd thought—I'd *hoped*—you were that person. What was it? Need help covering bills? Your ex leave you with no money? Or did you just count your lucky stars that you met a billionaire at your new job and thought this would be your ticket out of Vermont?"

He spun away from her.

"I don't care about your money."

He paused, keeping his back to her. "They all say that at first. It's not about the money. They like *me* for me. I don't believe it for one second, Sonora." He took a step. "If it wasn't about the money, you would have been honest with me up front."

"I wanted to."

"So what stopped you?" He half turned and imagined the glare he was giving her. He'd learned that from his father.

"Blythe is my best friend." Sonora took in a shaky breath. She stood next to the fire now, blanket fallen to the side. "She told me by accident and begged me not to say anything. She was…afraid."

"Of what?"

"You." Sonora bit her lip and dipped her chin. "You're a

powerful man, and if you'd learned that she'd accidentally breached the NDA, she could be in serious trouble. This is her dream job, and I just couldn't…I couldn't hurt her. I owe her a lot, and I thought it wouldn't matter."

"Well, it does."

"I see that now."

Were those tears in her eyes?

Graham looked away, his gaze seeking out the flames that mirrored the hot turmoil inside of him. He liked Sonora. Respected her and even admired her. But a maid? He didn't even know the first thing about cleaning a bathroom. How could they find common ground?

He shook his head, rubbing at the bridge of his nose. It didn't matter. This was it. She'd lied to him, and he was walking away.

Then why wasn't he moving?

"I mean it, Graham. I couldn't care if you had a thousand dollars to your name or five. Money means nothing to me. And I came out here…" Her voice broke. "I came here to tell you I care about you. I know we just met—I get how impossible it is—but I like you. I like the way you laugh at yourself and how you look to include others in whatever you're doing. And I like that you want to do things that matter. You care deeply, and I see that."

The fire in his chest dimmed but didn't die completely. Her words meant something to him. They hit at a spot he'd kept to himself—the one that craved understanding. How was it possible this woman had slipped past his defenses and reached into a part of him he thought no one would ever appreciate?

But she'd lied to him.

"I'm glad you do. You might be the only one." The truth was bitter on his cold lips. "I can't trust you though. I've had too many people slip into my life because of what I can do for them, not because of who I am. And I can't risk myself"—*my heart*—"like that anymore. Goodnight, Sonora."

The darkness enveloped him as he trudged back through the

snowy path to the resort. The further he got from the fire—from Sonora—the colder he became, and he couldn't ignore the analogy for his life.

She'd brought warmth to him, and he was choosing to walk into the cold. Without her.

TWENTY-SEVEN

THE COLD SANK into Sonora's bones, driven deeper by the look of betrayal on Graham's face. She'd expected him to be unhappy about what she had to say, but she hadn't expected the anger. Maybe she should have.

She shoved her hands under the blanket and leaned more closely to the dying fire. Embers ascended toward the darkness, and Sonora couldn't help but wish she was like them. Able to fly away to a new location at a moment's notice.

It wasn't that she *wanted* to leave Vermont so much as she wanted to escape her mistake. She should have owned up to who she was the minute Graham asked her out to coffee. Perhaps then none of this would be an issue. Blythe's job might have been in danger—it still could be—and that was one thing she did regret. She should have told her friend she was going to come clean to Graham, but Marcus' encouragement was all Sonora had needed to seek out the man she wanted to share the truth with.

"So the truth is out."

Sonora started, jerked back from her scrutiny of the flames. Blythe had a plaid shawl wrapped around her shoulders as she came to perch on the chair next to Sonora.

"I'm so sorry." Sonora searched her friend's face for the fallout of what she'd shared with Graham. She wouldn't be out here if he hadn't said something to her.

"Don't be. It was wrong of me to ask you to keep something from a guy you clearly like." Blythe sent her a pointed look. "But he did pop into my office to tell me I didn't have to worry."

Sonora's heart leapt. "Really? What did he say?"

"Not much." Blythe's expression softened even more. "He looked…focused."

"That sounds bad."

"It wasn't good." Blythe's nose scrunched. "But he said he understood why I'd made the mistake of sharing with you, and that he probably would have done the same if it were Marcus. I think he understands how deep our friendship is."

Blythe reached out and squeezed Sonora's hand.

"Still, I should have warned you I was going to tell him. I just had talked with Marcus and—"

"You did? What did he say?"

Sonora recounted the brief encounter with Graham's friend. "I'm pretty sure he knew the truth of who I am—perhaps he's known for a while now—and it felt like he wanted me to come clean before he had to tell Graham himself."

"That's fair, I guess."

"It was the right thing to do." *I should have done it sooner.*

"And I'm sorry for putting you in the position I did. Do you think Graham will come around?"

"You're assuming there's something for him to come around to."

"Isn't there?" Blythe cocked an eyebrow.

Sonora felt heat in her cheeks that had nothing to do with the fire. "Yeah. There is."

"That's a good thing, Sonora. You deserve someone who makes you happy."

"But he doesn't deserve someone like me." She flinched at the callousness in her own words.

"You and I both know that's not true."

"Who am I, B? I mean, really? I'm a woman who fled a difficult situation she got herself into, and here I am, cleaning hotel rooms for a living, in a state I know nothing about. And I spent a whole week lying to a handsome man who may never forgive me for deceiving him."

The situation sank in deeper then, dragging her shoulders down with it. One week. That's all it had taken for Graham to push his way past her walls and melt her once-broken heart. And she'd been the one to mess it up.

"Hope is not lost, my friend." Blythe nudged Sonora's knee. "If you'd seen him like I had, I'm sure you would feel the same way. He just needs time to process. There's no way the fact that you're a maid—*temporarily*, I might add—will prejudice him against you. And if it does, then good riddance to him."

Sonora laughed. "You sound like a grandma."

"Maybe I do, but I'm right either way. Sonora, open your eyes. He really likes you. I could tell, and I'm fairly certain he'll be back. Maybe not tonight, but surely before he leaves."

Before he leaves.

The fact Graham was leaving the next day had almost escaped her. How had she forgotten he wasn't staying indefinitely?

"What if he leaves and we never speak?"

"Don't let that happen." Blythe spoke like it was the easiest thing in the world to stop a man like Graham Hastings from doing anything he wanted.

"I'm not sure I have a choice."

"There's always a choice." Blythe stood, her smile as warm as the fire and as welcoming. "You, my friend, are not helpless. You never have been—even when you thought you were. You got yourself out of that relationship with Jonah, and you'll figure out a way to have a conversation with Graham. I know you can. I just expect a progress report when you do."

Sonora merely shook her head at her friend's confidence, but as Blythe walked back toward the lodge and light snowflakes began to fall, she wanted to hope that what her friend said was true.

For so long, she'd existed in the daily struggle of second-guessing herself. How she'd missed, or found excuses for, the signs of Jonah's control over her life was beyond her, but she'd gotten out, and that's what was important. That's what Blythe was reminding her.

There was always a tomorrow. Always a next step. Always a choice.

Sonora stood, already feeling the flakes growing in size and intensity. It was time to go back to her small cabin and relax in front of the gas fire with her journal. She had to do something to let out her thoughts and plan for a meeting tomorrow.

Maybe there was a way to have Marcus help her convince Graham to speak with her one last time. She had to show him that she truly didn't care about his money. That she only cared to know him better.

Her boots scuffed the snow covering the walkway, and any residual heat from the fire left her the further she went toward her cabin.

In the distance, she caught sight of headlights through the trees. It was most likely a car on the road that ran along the back of the Lodge's manicured property. It wound through the trees from the maintenance buildings and exited at a back gate to a side road. She'd only taken it once when she'd come back from town on an errand for Blythe, and it was usually closed to most motorists and not open to guests.

She vaguely wondered who could be coming in so late at night, but then she remembered it wasn't *that* late. The daylight left early each evening, and she'd gotten up early so the day had seemed much longer than normal.

Stifling a yawn, she took a left at the fork in the paths. If she'd gone right, it would have led to a small fish pond that was frozen over during the winter. She'd only gone that way once during the day and thought it would be a beautiful sight in the spring and summer.

The left fork took her to the four small cabins. Hers and three vacant ones. As she understood it, Blythe would fill them with extra staff in the summer, but the winter months usually left them empty. Sonora was just thankful she had a place to stay that she could call her own.

She adjusted the band on her wrist as she neared the door. It was surprising how quickly she'd become accustomed to the thing, even though it was cumbersome at times. Knowing she could get alerts and send alerts to the front desk when needed made the hassle worth it.

The bracelet touched the keypad of her door with a soft click. She moved her hand down to the handle when a voice spoke behind her.

"Hello, Sonora."

Every nerve ending came alive as her heart pounded in surprise. But the voice…it couldn't be.

She turned slowly, almost reluctantly, to face—

"Jonah."

TWENTY-EIGHT

"WHAT ARE YOU DOING HERE?"

Graham paced back and forth in front of the gas fireplace in the common room of the suite he shared with Marcus. "I needed time to think."

"No. You ran away." Marcus closed the lid of his laptop and leaned his elbows on his knees. "How are you supposed to work things out if you don't give her a chance?"

"A chance? We've known each other for a week, and she never thought to tell me some basic facts about herself?"

"You know the constraints of the retreat," Marcus countered.

"And you know she's not actually constrained by them."

Marcus nodded to the side. "Okay. True, but you still have to talk to her to figure things out."

"We did talk." Graham grimaced. It was more like her *trying* to tell him things but him not listening. "Sort of."

Graham felt the weight of his best friend's glare, but he stared out into the darkness of the window instead of facing him. He didn't feel like talking. In fact, he didn't feel like anything other than reading a book. Maybe that's what he should do. He could think about all of this emotional stuff later.

"Nope. You're not retreating into your book. You're going to hash this out with me."

Graham moved past Marcus, but his friend beat him to the punch, grabbing the book and shoving it behind him.

"You've got to be kidding me. What are we? Twelve? Hand over the book."

"Not until you tell me what's going on in that head up there."

Graham rolled his eyes. "You're not my therapist."

"Thank the Lord for that. Besides, I'm better than that. I'm your friend."

Graham sank into the leather armchair across from Marcus and dropped his face into his hands. "There's not much to tell. She told me she'd been lying to me, and she said a lot of nice things, but in the end, I know who she is. She's just like the rest of them, and I told her that."

Marcus let out a heavy sigh. "Smooth."

Graham jerked upright. "*I'm* the one who was lied to. I don't need to be smooth."

"What else did she say?" Marcus' words were calm. Controlled.

Graham wished he had some of that control. "She says she doesn't care about my money. Says she…likes me."

"That's good."

Graham shot a look across the room, but Marcus was all smiles. "Good?"

"You like her. She likes you. She's actually someone I'd approve of you dating and—"

"Wait. What? She lied to me—technically her best friend broke an NDA I could sue over—and…" He lost steam.

"See? That right there, my friend, is why you're blowing this out of proportion. I get it," Marcus held up his hands. "You were hurt, and you are justified in that feeling, but beyond that, there's nothing more keeping you two apart. Not now anyway."

"I could never trust her."

He felt rather than saw Marcus' studying look.

"I get women like Monique. Sure, she told me she liked me for me, but I think I always knew deep down, I would break up with her. She was the kind of woman I could take to parties but never had to take seriously." Graham ran a hand through his hair. "But Sonora…I knew she was different. I mean, I couldn't have guessed she was on the housekeeping staff, but I knew she was—*is*—a woman of substance."

"Then what's the problem? Surely you don't care about her working as a maid."

"No." Graham's answer was immediate "I don't care about that."

"Then what is it?" Marcus pushed.

"Sonora is the kind of woman I could see myself having a life with. A whole life, not some sort of on again, off again dating relationship. How can I think that about her, and she was able to lie to my face for a week straight? Doesn't that make something in me, I don't know, off?"

"It means you saw her for who she was, not her job title or situation." Marcus shrugged. "In all reality, what does it matter if she's staff or earning more than you do? Would you still like her if she had more money than you?"

"The money doesn't matter."

"Exactly. So why are you making it about that?"

"It's not that. It's the lie."

"Do you think she lied to you about anything else? That ex you mentioned before? Or her desire to do humanitarian work? Do you think those things were all lies?"

Graham paused before answering. He saw what his friend was doing, but he also appreciated it. He didn't think she'd lied about that. And, when he was honest with himself, he knew she never would have been in league with Craig Garrett. It was just something his wounded heart had prodded him with.

"No. I think that was all the truth."

"And why did she lie to you again?"

"Because she was protecting her friend."

Marcus' smug expression said he knew he was ahead in this conversation. It wasn't a competition, but if it was, Marcus would be winning.

"Man, I get it. It's never a good feeling to find out you were lied to, but don't let that keep you from something that could be really amazing. Take it from a guy who knows what it's like to fall in love."

"Kenna has really done a number on you." Graham grinned.

"She's pretty great. I only say all of this because I don't want you to miss out."

Graham nodded. His vision flooded with Sonora's gray eyes moist with tears. The way she'd pleaded with him to hear her words. The truth of what she was saying. She'd pointed to what she'd seen in him, and that cut through everything else. If he hadn't been so hurt, he might have seen her observations for what they were. Insight from someone who cared enough to look deeply into him.

There was no surface level with Sonora. She cared genuinely and gave freely of her time, encouragement, and even finances, as limited as they were.

He cringed, pushing to his feet to pace again. He'd said some terrible things to her. Unfair things. He needed to apologize and see if maybe there was hope for them to salvage…what? What was this that they'd started? It was too soon to call it a relationship, but he wanted that.

He wanted to be around her. Hear her laugh. Talk with her more about her ideas of helping those in Middlebrook and beyond.

"I need to go speak with her."

"Finally." Marcus leaned back, arms crossed. "See? Wasn't this better than reading?"

"Okay, in this instance, talking about my feelings with you was better than reading. But that's likely the last time you'll ever hear those words coming out of this mouth. Now, where is she?"

Marcus frowned.

"I know you. I know you did your homework, probably long before you clued me in on her, and you already know where her room is."

The corner of Marcus' lips twitched up. "Not a room. She's got a cabin at the back of the grounds. It's aptly named *Mistletoe*."

"You're kidding."

"Not even one bit."

Graham reached for his coat and headed toward the door.

"Hey."

He turned, and a black beanie smacked him in the face. His quick reflexes meant he caught it before it dropped to the floor.

"Thanks, man." Graham infused the words with meaning that went beyond the hat, and Marcus knew it.

"I won't wait up."

Graham laughed and left the room for the quiet of the hallway.

He turned toward the exit as he slipped into his jacket and yanked the beanie down over his hair. Cold swirls of snow pelted him as he left the warmth of the hallway and entered the night.

A tiny cyclone of nerves coiled in his abdomen at the thought of talking with Sonora again. He needed to apologize—that was first on the list. But then what? What could he say? What would *she* say? What was next for them?

He shook his head as a snowflake landed on his eyelashes. He blinked it away and tried to center his thoughts on the simple fact that, once the confusion of the past week was behind them, they could start this again. Whatever this was.

The small lights that illuminated the already-snowy pathway led him toward the cabins he'd barely given a second thought to. He'd initially thought they might be private guest cottages, but now it made sense they were set apart for staff who stayed on the property.

He reached a small wooden bridge that was slick with snow and ice. Crossing that, he was greeted with a sign that offered directions to four cabins. Huckleberry, Mistletoe, Hemlock, and Blackberry.

Taking the direction the arrow pointed, he set off for Mistletoe. His hands ached with cold despite the fact they were nestled in his pockets, but soon, he found the cabin with Mistletoe engraved on a wooden sign above the door. A small drawing of what he assumed was mistletoe accompanied the text. It was cute, and he half-expected there to be a bundle of mistletoe over the door, but he had no such luck.

His hand shifted from pocket to door before hovering there, growing more frozen by the second.

Come on. Knock, you coward.

His knuckles met wood in a hollow sounding thud.

Knock. Knock, Knock.

He waited. After almost a whole minute, he repeated the process but still with no result. He pursed his lips leaning toward the minimal warmth the shelter of her doorway offered. Had he miscalculated? Was it possible she was still inside?

He thought back to the night he'd found her in the kitchen. It wasn't as late as it had been then, but there was a possibility she'd gone in search of a midnight snack.

Turning his back on her door, he hurried back over the bridge and toward the lodge's entrance. He was going to find her, no matter what. They needed to talk, and if at all possible, he wanted it to be tonight.

It was either that, or he wasn't sleeping until the next day.

TWENTY-NINE

"JONAH, WHY ARE YOU HERE?" Sonora fought to keep her teeth from chattering. She didn't want to show him how uncomfortable she was, but that would only last so long. Her entire body threatened to break into uncontrollable shaking—from fear and cold—if she didn't get out of there soon.

Seeing Jonah in Vermont was the furthest thing she'd expected, but when he escorted—half-dragged—her to one of the unoccupied cabins and pushed the door in, the chill of fear that raced up her spine had nothing to do with the cold outside.

"I missed you." He stood in front of the gas fireplace, the only thing that illuminated the cabin.

She swallowed down the words she wanted to say and reached for tact. "We ended our relationship months ago. You don't get to just show up like this, and you know that."

"See, that's the thing. *You're* the one that wanted to end things, but I didn't agree to it."

Sonora fought the ill-timed urge to laugh at the absurdity of it all. "It was my choice to make." She tried, and failed, to infuse her voice with certainty.

"What makes you think your choice trumps mine?"

She shifted away from his intent gaze and stared into the fire, wishing it was the same fire she'd shared with Graham only a few hours before.

Where was Graham? Was he all right? She hoped so. She hoped he could forgive her.

A memory of what she'd told him came back to her, and it reminded her that she *had* a choice. With Jonah and in this situation.

She stood. "I appreciate the fact you wanted to be here to work things out in person, but I don't think—no, I *know* that's not possible. We're done, Jonah. I'm not marrying you, and I'm sorry, but I want you out of my life."

Facing him eye to eye, the same rush of fear washed through her. He'd never done anything to her physically, but the control he had enacted over her was its own kind of manacle. The threat of being under that control again sent spikes of anxiety through her, and she took an involuntary step back.

"You don't get to push me out, SJ. You just don't." He acted like there wasn't a care in the world, but she knew the minute she took a step toward the door, he'd intercept her. Still, she had to try.

She moved, and he mirrored her actions.

"Not so fast, SJ. We're not done talking."

Hope spluttered and died. There were two ways out of this. One, she sat and talked with him, and the other, she fought him for freedom. She might win if they tried to wrestle for the door, but she didn't relish the reality that she might not win as well.

"I'll stay and hear you out," she said. "But then I'm leaving, and you're going to let me go."

Her words were calculated to test the waters. She needed to show Jonah that she was no longer the same woman who would lie down and take his demands. She wasn't the same woman he'd asked to marry him.

His eyes narrowed, but he nodded once. "I'm confident that, once I've made my case, you'll see things my way. But sure, if you want to leave after that, okay."

She caught the tick in his jaw. The one that said he wasn't being honest. "Okay. Then talk."

Sonora sat back down and prayed that the night security guard would notice the firelight and investigate. Short of a miracle, that was the only way she was getting out of this cabin a free woman.

THIRTY

"DUDE, why are you back so early?" Marcus looked up from where he sat on the couch with his computer.

Graham heard another voice and realized he'd interrupted a video call between Marcus and his girlfriend.

"Sorry, Kenna," he called out. "I need a moment with Marcus."

"No problem." Her reply came over the laptop speakers.

"Sorry, babe. I'll call you back." Marcus closed the laptop, and Graham met him halfway into the room.

"I can't find her."

"Sonora?"

"No, Mrs. Claus. Yes, Sonora."

Marcus offered an unamused look his way before pulling on his shoes.

"I went to her cabin, and a light was on, but no one was home." Unless she'd been ignoring him. But his gut pinched with the thought that it was something other than that. Something more pressing. He just didn't know what.

"You checked the gym?" Marcus pulled on a hooded sweatshirt.

"Yeah. And the pool, library, game room, and hot chocolate bar."

"What about the—"

"Kitchen? It was the first place I looked."

Marcus frowned. "Maybe we should talk to Blythe."

"Good idea."

Both men pushed into the hall and headed for the main lobby area. It was quiet, Graham's watch saying it was just after eleven at night. He'd been looking for her for almost forty-five minutes. While the resort was big, it wasn't *that* big. He should have found her by now.

"It's okay, man. Maybe she and Blythe are doing a girls movie night or something."

The idea instantly relaxed Graham's shoulders. That was a good possibility. She and Blythe were best friends, and girls watched movies when they had boy troubles, right? He had no idea, but it sounded like something they might do.

"Yeah. Good idea. I guess we'll just ask at the front desk."

His attention snapped in the direction of the front desk just as Blythe rounded the desk and stopped in her tracks. "Graham."

"What's wrong?" He could instantly tell she was worried or nervous, something about her usually poised expression that hinted at it.

"I just got an alert from our security guy." Blythe bit her lip. "Someone came in at the South Gate a half an hour ago. I—I haven't had a chance to hire someone new for that gate, and no one ever uses it, and I thought it would be okay."

"Hey, it's all right." Graham gently cupped her upper arm in a show of support. "Tell us what happened."

She told them about the footage the front gate security guard had sent to her after a motion alert triggered his attention. She said he'd had to go back through the logs to find the video, but a man in a dark SUV had come in and hadn't left yet.

Graham's gut churned more violently. "I can't find Sonora."

Blythe's complexion mirrored the snow. "What?"

"I looked everywhere. I thought she might be with you."

"No. I talked with her outside after…" Blythe blushed. "After you and I talked. But I'm positive she was going to her cabin. We'll just check there."

"I did. I mean, she could have not answered the door because it was me, but I don't think so. I don't think she was there."

"Oh no. Do you think…could it be Jonah?" Blythe's hand moved to cover her lips, her fingers trembling.

"Would she be in her cabin *with* him?"

"Not willingly." Blythe took deep breaths. "I don't know how much she's told you, but he's a very controlling person and did not take her breaking off their engagement well."

Graham nodded. "I'm aware."

"And you know about the flowers and the text?"

Graham started to nod but stopped. "Text?"

"Yes. He got her new number somehow. I honestly don't know how he does it, but I think he has a lot of connections with law enforcement in Louisiana."

"So he was stalking her." Marcus looked between them.

"She'd put it that way, though she did try to downplay it," Graham said.

"I only met him once before they got engaged. I thought he was a nice guy." Blythe reached up to push her hair back and paused when her eyes landed on her wrist. "Oh! Her bracelet. What was I thinking?"

Graham frowned. "What?"

"The bracelets." Blythe held up her arm and pointed to the silicone band with a round disc on one side. "They have location trackers."

"Really?" Marcus frowned. "That seems kind of…controlling."

"Come on." Blythe waved them to follow. "I know, it's strange. We just got them this year, per my grandfather's direction, which is why I didn't think of it. I keep forgetting about them."

"I don't understand. What do they do?"

"It's a way for us to contact the employees and to locate them."

She shared a story about an employee who'd gotten lost in a blizzard, and Graham began to understand their necessity.

"You can find her through her bracelet?" Graham asked.

"I should be able to. As long as she's still on the resort property."

Graham's stomach knotted at the thought that she might not be. But Blythe had said her security guy hadn't seen the vehicle leave, so he was holding on to that.

Blythe rounded the desk in her office and tapped a key on her keyboard to wake up her computer. She slid into her seat and called up a desktop app that showed a set of twelve circles. He assumed they represented staff. When she clicked on one, he saw the name below read Sonora.

Hoping this was going to be the break they needed, he watched as Blythe tapped the "locate" button. The minute she did, the screen shifted and gave way to an overview map of the lodge. It was clearly high-tech and done well with each landmark noted in bold letters

"There. She's," Blythe leaned forward, "in Hemlock. What?"

"What's that?" Marcus asked.

"One of the cabins," Graham supplied. He remembered the signs. "Come on." He moved toward the door, but Blythe stopped him.

"Wait. Graham—we have to have a game plan here. I think I need to call the authorities."

"I'm not leaving her alone with that guy." His hand connected with the door handle. "I'm going."

"Okay. Yeah. Just take this." She fumbled in her desk and came up with another wrist band. After tapping a few keys, she scanned the band across a black pad, and it beeped. "Hemlock is closed down for the winter, or it should be, so I don't know how he got in there, but this will give you access."

"Thanks." He caught the bracelet as she tossed it.

"I'll call the police and meet them at the gate to direct them." Blythe stood and started to pull on her coat and fur-lined boots.

"We'll keep her safe," Marcus said.

Graham turned back and saw what his friend had. Blythe's fear for Sonora. Graham had been so focused on getting to Sonora, he hadn't caught that.

"We will, Blythe. Promise." He added his sentiments and then rushed out the door, Marcus quick on his heels.

THIRTY-ONE

SONORA WAS SHIVERING NOW. While it seemed like the electricity to the cabin had been cut off, the gas fireplace still worked. It was helpful but did little against the prevailing chill that took over the space. Whether Jonah didn't notice it or didn't care, she wasn't sure, but he didn't seem affected.

Instead, he paced back and forth, going on and on about how she needed to come back to Louisiana. She'd about had enough of it but wasn't sure what he would do if she interrupted him.

"All of that to say," he rounded on her, "it's time for you to come back."

He had said some form of this for the last half an hour, and her response had been the same. "I'm staying here."

"Ugh. Sonora!" His shout made her flinch. "What does Vermont have that we don't have back in NOLA? Tell me that."

She wanted to say, *it doesn't have you*, but refrained. Instead, she did something she hadn't had the confidence or control to do before. She stood and faced him.

"I'm not going back with you. I'm staying in Vermont, and this is why." She took a deep breath of the frigid air. "I don't love you. At first, I thought I did, and I convinced myself that you truly cared for me. That all of the ways you tried to control me were due to your love for me, but that's not love."

She paced closer to the fire for the vestige of warmth it would offer. "Love offers freedom and support. Love says that my opinion matters in our relationship, not just yours. And love doesn't try and force its own way."

"You don't know what love is."

"I know it's not this. What are you doing here, Jonah?"

"I came to bring you back. I let you stay with Donna when I found out that's where you were, but only because I hoped it would help you figure out whatever it is that's confusing you. But then you left—without telling me, mind you—and I had to track you down. Isn't *that* love? I hired a private plane to get me up here, and it's going to take us back. We'll get married, and then I'm taking you on that trip to Austria you always talked about."

She frowned. She'd never talked about going to Austria. "No. I'm not going."

He took a step toward her, but there was no menace, only desperation. "Sonora, you're going to be my wife. Why are you doing this? Pushing me away like this?"

He couldn't understand. She didn't know why, but he couldn't accept that she wouldn't choose to stay with him.

"No, Jonah. I'm done."

She moved to step around him, but he blocked her path. "Is it someone else? Is that why you're up here?"

"No." Though, as she said the words, an image of Graham came to mind. Yes, there was the possibility of someone else, but even that had failed.

Maybe it was better for her to be alone.

"I'm going, Jonah. Let us part ways on good terms and—"

"No." He stepped closer, and his hand wrapped protectively around her upper arm. "You've never believed me when I said I know what's best for you, but I do."

His voice sent a chill through her. His grip, while not painful, was ever-present, and she knew he would tighten it if she tried to pull away.

A plan began to form in her mind, one that spoke of desperation, but it was all she had.

THIRTY-TWO

GRAHAM NEARLY SLIPPED and fell as he raced across the bridge toward Hemlock cabin. Marcus wasn't so lucky and landed with a grunt on the ice-caked bridge.

"You okay?"

"Go." He held up a hand. "I'll be there in a second."

Graham could tell his friend wasn't seriously injured, but a fall like that on hard ice never felt good.

"I think it's just ahead on the right."

"Go," Marcus said again.

And Graham did. He raced down the sidewalk. The snow had stopped, but there was almost an inch on the existing path. He silently thanked the groundskeepers for keeping the sidewalks shoveled. It made the route clear and allowed him more speed, though his tennis shoes were no match for slippery snow.

The cabin appeared ahead, and he double checked the name above the door. Just like with Mistletoe, it had a carved image, this one of spindly flowers. He slowed his pace as he approached. The windows looked mostly dark, but in the complete darkness of the woods behind the cabin, he could tell there was a light on inside.

Sonora.

His gut clenched, and he slowed. What was the best approach here? As he narrowed in on the cabin, the doorknob twisted.

Unsure if it was best to charge forward or hang back to take stock of the situation, he did the latter, thinking it would allow him to see the dynamic of what was going on. It was possible Sonora could get herself away from her ex in a calm manner, and he didn't want to mess that up.

"I'm not going with you, Jonah." Sonora's voice had a brittle quality to it that sent shockwaves of fear through Graham.

This was not a calm situation. He could see that now from where he stood in the darkness, just outside the path lights.

A tall, well-built man had his hand around her upper arm and seemed to be almost carrying her down the steps of the cabin. It was clear from the distressed look on her face that she was not okay with how he was handling her.

That was Graham's cue. "Let her go."

Jonah froze, and Sonora's gaze shot to him. "Graham."

"You know this guy?" Jonah's voice had a harsh clip to it that spoke of someone who was accustomed to authority.

Graham knew the type and knew from the expression of fear on Sonora's face that this was a tenuous situation. One that Graham never expected to be in. He'd come to this retreat to find himself—to find his purpose—instead he was here, in the frigid cold, wanting to rescue Sonora with everything inside of him. He wanted her safe.

"This is Graham. He's a…friend."

Her slight hesitation gave Graham a strange boost of ego. It was clear from the expression on Jonah's face he'd caught it too. "I thought you said there was no one else."

"We've only just met," she said. Graham noted her casual avoidance of the true question, but unfortunately, Jonah did as well.

"I can't believe this."

Jonah's grip must have tightened if the flinch of Sonora's expression was any indication. Graham took another step forward.

"Hi. You must be her ex-fiancé." He purposefully used the term in order to get under the man's skin. "I'm Graham Hastings."

His name had the intended effect, and Jonah's confusion clouded. "The billionaire?"

"Yes."

"What are you doing in a dump like this?"

Sonora shifted, and Graham guessed she wanted to defend Blythe. Thankfully, she stayed quiet.

"I'm on vacation. I'm assuming that wasn't why you came here?" Graham needed to keep him talking while he thought of a plan. It didn't seem like Jonah was armed with any kind of weapon—a small mercy—but he was clearly emotionally unstable. His eyes darted back and forth from the mountains to Sonora to Graham and back in an endless skitter.

"I'm taking my wife back with me. That's why I'm here."

Graham caught the widening of Sonora's eyes.

"Wife? You were only ever engaged and she broke it off."

"Why does Graham Hastings know so much about our history, *babe*?" Jonah half-turned Sonora so he could look into her eyes.

Graham's pulse raced. Should he rush them? Was taking the man by surprise the best approach? He didn't want to risk Sonora getting hurt in the mix-up, but he also wanted her away from Jonah and his seeming need for control over her and her life.

"How about we all go inside and talk this out? Maybe over some hot chocolate?"

"I'm taking her back to Louisiana. I've chartered a plane. Just let us go in peace."

"I'm not going with you." Sonora's voice had a thin quality to it, but Graham could see the determined set of her jaw.

"We talked about this. It's almost Christmas, and we just need to go back where we've got friends and family. You know my parents want to see you for Christmas Eve dinner."

"I'm not going." Sonora sounded more resolute, and Graham took a subtle step forward.

He was contemplating his next move when Sonora shifted into action. She jammed her free elbow into Jonah's stomach while simultaneously breaking his hold by yanking her arm up and out of his grasp.

Jonah regained his footing easily enough and reached out for her, but Marcus appeared from the shadows, allowing her to slip past.

"Not so fast, buddy."

Jonah came up short. "Who are you?"

"I'm his best friend, and I also know Krav Maga. You don't want to cross me."

Jonah took one step forward, his eyes darting after Sonora, as blue and red lights brightened the dark woods. The authorities Blythe had called were here.

"Graham?" Sonora stood halfway between him and Jonah.

"It's okay, Sonora."

As if that was the invitation she needed, Sonora rushed the rest of the way to him, slipping into Graham's arms. Her hands fisted the front of his shirt under his unzipped coat as she ducked her head against his chest. He pulled her close, unable to ignore how her whole body shook. She was terrified and cold.

"Come on, let's get you inside where it's warm," he said.

"But—Jonah."

He looked down, trying to understand what she was saying, but the fear reflected in her eyes was all the answer he needed. She didn't want Jonah coming back for her, but that wasn't going to happen.

Graham looked up and met Jonah's gaze. Jonah's jaw flexed as he ground his teeth, eyes flicking between Marcus and Graham, clearly considering whether he could get past them both in time to break Sonora free and escape.

Graham hardened his gaze to let the man know it was never going to happen. "Marcus—"

"On it."

It was all Graham needed to know. He dipped his head, dropping his voice for her alone. "Marcus will stay until the police come. Come on." He held her close, and they took the slippery bridge with slow, careful steps. He directed them to the side door of the lodge and toward a small reading alcove close to the hot chocolate bar, with its own gas fireplace and floor to ceiling window. "Is here okay?"

She nodded, her lips a shade close to blue.

"Do you need a doctor?" Graham pulled a chair close to the fire and gently urged her to sit down as he took a spot on the ledge of the fireplace across from her.

"I'll b-b-be okay." She swallowed, her hands shoved deep into her pockets. "He kept me in that empty cabin for a while, and I got so cold."

"That and the shock, I'm sure. Are you positive you don't want me to get someone to take a look at you? I think Blythe said there was a nurse?"

"I'll be okay, Graham."

At the sound of his name on her lips, he relaxed some. She already looked better, some color coming into her cheeks. His back was to the fire, and he could admit the heat had a calming effect.

"Want to talk about it?"

Sonora peered into the flames and took in a deep breath before letting it flow out in a huff. "I don't know."

"You don't have to if you don't want to," he assured her. "It's your past and none of my business."

She shot him a look, and he realized what he'd said. Before he could explain, she began talking. "I'm sorry, Graham. For all of it. I know you probably can't understand why I did what I did, but I promise you it wasn't out of anything other than loyalty to Blythe."

Graham reached out and took her hands in his. They were like ice, so he rubbed them gently. "You don't have anything to apologize for."

"But I do."

"No." Graham focused his gaze on her hands for a moment longer before meeting her eyes. The gray reminded him of the sky on a cloudy morning that promised a storm. He loved storms. "No, I owe you an apology. I let my own hurt get in the way. It wasn't so much your omission that hurt, but the fact that I like you and didn't want to think I'd misjudged someone—again."

Compassion swelled, and she squeezed his hands back, her fingers wrapping around his. The glow of the fire and the small Christmas tree in the corner of the nook added a softness to the moment that pushed Graham closer. His gaze flickered to her lips.

"I'm sorry I didn't tell you the truth right away." She leaned forward. "I wanted to, but then I was afraid. I mean…I'm a maid. *Your* maid."

He frowned. "What?"

"I came to your room to clean." At his blank look, she persisted. "You were on the phone—maybe with your father? I was terrified that was the moment you'd know I'd been keeping so much from you, but…you didn't even recognize me."

A pit landed in his stomach, a heavy weight. "I'm sorry."

"I don't say that to shame you, just that I don't know how to fit into your world. I mean, not that I have to." She blushed and looked down.

He reached forward and finally let himself do what he'd wanted. He used a hooked knuckle to gently bring her chin up until she met his gaze.

"But what if I want you in my world?" He let the words rest between them before he leaned forward, and their lips met.

THIRTY-THREE

SONORA WAS SO surprised when Graham kissed her that she pulled back. His eyes flashed open, and she watched as his brow furrowed.

"I'm so sorry—"

She cut off his apology by pulling him close until their lips met again, prepared for the contact now. As she sank into the kiss, she tried and failed to silence the questions. The ones that asked how they could find common ground. How a romance that began at a lodge in Vermont could grow into anything.

When they pulled back, she bit her lip. Graham tasted sweet, like white chocolate and cinnamon, and the way his eyes melted as they took her in caused warmth to flood through her despite the cold at her core from Jonah's attempt to take her back with him.

"Sonora, I don't know what this is, but I want to give it time to grow." Graham spoke her own thoughts to her, and she dared to hope.

"I don't know how to do…this." She motioned between them. "Not you," she rushed to explain. "Just, a relationship. I've still got a lot of fear after what happened with Jonah."

She could tell Graham knew she wasn't talking about what had happened that night but the past. Her history with the controlling man.

"Then you're in good company because I still have a lot I'm unpacking from my past relationships—clearly." He chuckled and reached up to brush her hair back behind her ear. "I don't know how to do this either, but I want to try."

The words were too good to be true. It was like the tale of a young woman wandering into an enchanted forest only to come out the other side as a princess. These were the things of dreams, not reality.

But the man before her with his kind brown eyes and easy smile was real. She leaned forward and cupped his cheeks, his beard scratchy against her palms.

"I want to try too." The words were simple, but their meaning to her was deeper than anything she'd experienced before. Deeper than her attraction to Jonah back before she knew his true nature, and deeper than her fear.

This man had come after her to rescue her. He'd seen her heart despite not seeing her circumstance, and while it was going to take time for them to figure those things out, she knew one thing for certain. She wanted to try.

This time, he leaned forward to kiss her, and her hands slipped to his neck. She had to lean forward to meet him and she felt his hands rest lightly on her knees.

The flames flickered, and she felt her heart melt further at the tender way he kissed her. The gentleness of his lips on hers, the safety she felt being close to him, and the knowledge that he wasn't someone who was going to push her to do anything. She trusted him, and while that trust was fledgling, it would grow. Or so she hoped.

"There you are."

Sonora jerked back from Graham, her cheeks heating beneath the amused stare of her best friend. "Hi, Blythe."

"The sheriff needs a word with you, Sonora. That is, if you can be spared." Blythe shifted to spear Graham with a look that warned him he better treat her best friend with all the care he could.

"I can go with you." Graham was on his feet in an instant, hand held out to her. She accepted, and he pulled her easily to her feet, but he didn't let go of her hand.

"I'll go with her." Blythe speared Graham with another look. This one more assessing.

"What do you want, Sonora?" he asked.

The simple question was enough to send tears to Sonora's eyes. Concern furrowed Graham's brow, but she smiled to assure him she was all right.

"I'll be all right with Blythe, I promise."

"Of course." There wasn't even a hint of hesitation.

She turned to go with Blythe but paused when he called out to her friend.

"Blythe, you wouldn't happen to have availability for my suite for the rest of the year, would you?"

Sonora's eyes widened. That was another two weeks. She checked herself mentally, remembering that Graham could buy the hotel if he wanted, never mind a two-week stay. It wasn't that so much as it was the time away from the business matters he likely had to attend to. Would he really be able to stay that long?

"I'll see what I can do for you, Mr. Hastings." She flashed a smile as she whispered his last name, then reached for Sonora, pulling her close.

They left Graham in the alcove and headed toward the lobby and Blythe's office, or so Sonora assumed.

"That was unexpected," Blythe said. She turned her gaze toward Sonora for a moment before leaving her to answer.

"I think he's forgiven me for lying." Both women burst into laughter as they entered the lobby, but they both stifled it quickly.

Sonora never would have thought there was anything to be joyful about after the horrible encounter she'd had with Jonah, but laughing with her best friend was good medicine.

Blythe pulled her to a stop before they entered her office.

"Sheriff O'Brian is a great guy and a wise man. He actually used to work in New York but wanted a slower pace of life, so you don't have to worry that he's going to be incompetent or anything. I gave him a brief rundown of your relationship with Jonah, but he'll need to hear it from you, naturally. I think he needs to know the best course of action."

"I don't know what that is." Sonora shifted from one foot to another.

"He'll know. Just be honest with him." Blythe held her gaze. "I'll be there the whole time, too. Okay?"

Sonora nodded, and the women walked into the office. Sheriff O'Brian sat at one of the chairs with another deputy standing by the door.

"Please, have a seat, Ms. Jackson. I'm sure Blythe has told you all about me, but I'm Roger O'Brian, sheriff of Middlebrook. We've got your ex-fiancé in a cruiser, and he'll be taken off the property for trespassing, but what you say determines what else he could be charged with. Why don't you start from the top and tell me what happened tonight?"

Sonora did, starting with the walk to her cabin and how he'd grabbed her from behind and forced her to the unoccupied cabin. She gave vague details about what they had talked about, getting to the heart of it all with his determination to get her back to Louisiana with him.

"I'm guessing you don't want to go back with him. Do I have that right?"

"Correct." Sonora looked down at her hands, wishing Graham were here to hold them again. "I don't want him in my life anymore. I've told him that repeatedly, but he doesn't seem to understand."

"Gotcha." The sheriff made a few notes in a notebook and asked several more probing questions about her past life with Jonah. They were uncomfortable, especially having Blythe there, but her friends' eyes only held compassion.

Admitting that Jonah had convinced her not only to give up

her plans for the future but also her innocence held the sting of shame. He'd all but demanded she be his wife in every aspect and, at the time, she'd seen no way to say no to him. He was the one who held the keys to their future—all but literally.

After the confession, a weight lifted with the gentle squeeze of Blythe's arms around her and the compassion in the sheriff's gaze.

"Ma'am, you've endured more than most with this guy. And before you go on telling me that he didn't lay a hand on you, there is more than one type of abuse. You've escaped, and we're going to do what we can to ensure your safety."

Sonora was positive they could see her floating. The effect of the sheriff's understanding and compassion made her believe a new life was possible.

After the paperwork was completed and he asked her to come by the police station the next day to officially sign the restraining order against Jonah, he said she was free to go.

"Sonora." Blythe slipped her arm around Sonora's shoulders as they exited the station.

The weight of her name on Blythe's lips broke her, and she dissolved into tears. "I feel so foolish."

"Wait, what?" Blythe pulled her into a hug. "You have nothing to feel ashamed about."

"I knew I needed to leave but I didn't."

"Don't be so hard on yourself. You made excuses for his controlling nature, and I understand why. You thought the best of him and did what you could to make things work, but you *did* eventually leave. I'm just glad it's behind you."

Sonora took in a shuddering breath. "It is. Behind me, that is. Isn't it?"

"It is." Blythe looked behind her as they exited the front desk area. "And I think someone wants to see you again. I better go book out his rooms for the next two weeks." Blythe moved to step past her but paused to whisper, "Somebody likes you."

Nervous butterflies flooded Sonora's stomach as she turned to see Graham striding toward her, focused on her like a ship narrowing in on a homing beacon. His laser focus was on her, and she sensed the same tug toward him. They met in front of the towering Christmas tree, and he wrapped her in his arms.

The fragrance of fir needles and cinnamon enveloped her along with Graham's woodsy scent, and it felt like coming home.

How was it possible he knew she needed this? Needed him after such a short time? Was this something that could last, or had Sonora convinced herself there was a future past the magic of Christmas lights and falling snow?

As she pulled back and looked into Graham's eyes, the golden lights of the towering tree reflected there, along with her own questions.

THIRTY-FOUR

GRAHAM REACHED up and traced a finger down Sonora's cheek. The last few hours had simultaneously been a waking nightmare and a dream come true. Standing with her here now in front of the Christmas tree, its golden lights shimmering against the darkness of the windows behind, was the perfect contrast to how the night had started.

Light cast out fear, and love shone brightest of all.

Love. Was it possible he was already in love with Sonora? His eyes searched her soft features, more familiar to him by the day, and he knew it wasn't infatuation or some type of holiday crush. They'd been brought together for a reason, and now that he'd found her, he didn't want to let her go.

"Sonora." He whispered her name as a promise.

Her lips tilted upward, and he desperately wanted to kiss her again but knew now was not the time. Those emotions and feelings, wonderful as they were, would only complicate things. He didn't want her to think he was interested in her for anything other than who she was at the core.

"I meant what I said before. I want to know what you like to do on the weekends and what your favorite color is. I want to laugh more with you and learn about your past—the good and the bad." He stopped himself before he went on. There were so many things about this woman he craved to know. "I guess what I'm saying is, I want to give us a shot."

His hand brushed down her arm to find her hand. Her fingers intertwined with his, and he felt how real she was. This was no dream. Not fantasy magic that would fade after you put the book down. It was reality, and he wanted all of it. With her.

"Blue."

He frowned. "Uh, what?"

"My favorite color is blue. I love to sleep in late and read by the fire on the weekends. My dad left when I was six, and my mom…well, she's a topic for another day, but it's a start."

He searched her eyes, but she went on.

"I have a lot of fear from the past—from Jonah—but I don't want that to stop what's happening here." She pressed her palm to his chest. "You have a good heart, Graham Hastings, and I want to know the same things you do."

"Red." He inched closer. "Ditto on the weekend reading, though occasionally, I like to go for long drives through the countryside when possible. And my dad's a piece of work, but I'm doing everything I can to grow into the man he should have been."

Silence blanketed them like the snow falling outside as Graham leaned down to lightly press his lips to hers. "Come to the dinner with me?" he asked.

"Yes." Her answer was instantaneous.

The joy that filled him in that moment was otherworldly and reminded him of the best scenes from books he'd always loved. The same feeling of excitement and anticipation that captivated him reached into his life now with the promise that there was more on the horizon. And that it was going to be better than anything he could have imagined.

THIRTY-FIVE

SONORA RAN her hands down the velvety red fabric of her dress as she stared back at her reflection in the mirror. The sweetheart neckline descended to ruching that gathered at the waist before dropping to the floor in a slimming line. It hugged her curves and exposed her left leg starting at just above the knee. But her favorite part were the red lace sleeves that added a touch of warmth.

"You look *amazing*!" Blythe, sheathed in her own midnight blue dress, peered over her shoulder.

"I can't believe Graham had this delivered." Sonora blushed. "You really think it looks okay? It's not…too much?"

"Girl." Blythe gently turned her around until they were facing each other. "You are stunning. And I'm not just talking about the dress. You've changed in the last few days, more like you used to be in college, and it's a good thing. I'm so happy for you."

Sonora frowned in thought. "I think it was something about what Sheriff O'Brian said. That Jonah won't be a problem any longer. It gave me the freedom I needed to remember who I used to be. Without him."

"I can't imagine the fear you lived in." Blythe's compassion spilled over. "I should have known something was up. I'm sorry." She leaned forward, enveloping Sonora in a warm hug.

"Don't apologize. Jonah's the one to blame. I see that now." She pulled back. "You were right. I put the pressure on myself, but that was never fair. I was like a frog in hot water, not knowing I was boiling alive until it was too late."

"You mean *almost* too late." Blythe's eyes shimmered with tears. "And now it's like you've kissed your own frog."

Sonora burst out laughing. "Graham is *not* a frog."

"But he sure is a prince charming." Blythe winked but sobered quickly. "I'm so happy for you. You deserve this kind of happiness."

Sonora bit her lip, looking down where her hands fumbled with the edge of the lace at her wrist. "How will it all work?"

"You mean you and him?"

Sonora nodded. She'd experienced such a freedom the first few days after Jonah's arrest. She and Graham had taken snowy walks, a sleigh ride, and gone back to town for another coffee date, but then she'd woken up this morning, on Christmas Eve, to a barrage of worry.

"We're from such different worlds. He lives in LA. I'm in Vermont now. How does that work?"

Blythe considered her, head tilting to the side. "You'll find a way."

Her confident answer was a flicker of hope. "But *how*?"

"Flights. Calls. Texts. Who knows? The main thing is do you *want* it to work?"

"Yes." At least that answer was easy.

"Then the rest will fall into place." Blythe reached out and squeezed her shoulder. "I'm no expert on love, but I think it can overcome some of the greatest of barriers. It's not to say there won't be hard times, but you find a way to make it work. At least that's what my sisters say."

Sonora laughed, picturing Blythe's three older sisters. They had all been married for years by now, and she could see their influence in Blythe's understanding of marriage.

"I think I'm just nervous." Sonora shook out her hands.

"Just remember"—Blythe leaned in—"he's the same guy you met over hot cocoa when you didn't know his last name, and he had no idea you were a maid. *That's* who you both are at the core."

"Thanks, B."

"Of course. Now, let's get you to the party. Your Prince Charming awaits."

THIRTY-SIX

GRAHAM'S VISION tunneled as he looked up and caught sight of Sonora descending the staircase to the ballroom. The red dress he'd had delivered to her that morning fit like a glove, accentuating her womanly figure in the most appealing way.

It was her gaze though, fixed on him with such intensity, that held him captivated. Anticipation mingled with happiness—and matched his own feelings.

If someone would have told him he'd be waiting for the most beautiful woman to join him for dinner and dancing on Christmas Eve, he would have laughed in their faces, but here she was.

She reached the bottom step, and he moved forward, hand outstretched to her. When her hand slipped into his, the fit was perfect. She was perfect.

"You look beautiful." He took a step back, admiring the gown from top to bottom and back again.

"Look." She grinned and spun so he could see the back.

The red lace descended in a V to the gathered waist, and he held back the urge to run a hand over the smooth skin of her back.

"Very nice," he said instead.

She spun back, excitement in her eyes. "You didn't have to get this for me."

"I know. I *wanted* to."

"I haven't ever worn anything so nice." Her hands smoothed the velvet at her waist. "Thank you, Graham."

"You're welcome, Sonora." He gently pulled her closer and relished the way her eyes softened as they met his.

He already knew more about her than he had a few days before, but it wasn't enough. He wasn't sure if it would ever be enough. He craved time with her, and when they were apart, all he could think about was her.

"You look serious," she said. Reaching up, Sonora smoothed two fingers lightly across his brow.

He laughed. "Sorry. I was just thinking…"

"About?" she pressed.

"You. Us. This." He took in a deep breath. "Dance with me?"

"Yes."

Her quick answer made him smile, and he guided her out onto the dance floor. Several other couples were already dancing, and the music shifted to *Silver Bells*.

"I love Bing Crosby." Sonora smiled up at him.

"What else do you love?" The question slipped out, and he rushed to explain. "I mean, like music." Was he blushing?

Sonora laughed, her eyes glinting from the strings of Christmas lights crossing above them from the exposed rafters of the ballroom. "I love chocolate cake, puppies, and old movies. What about you?"

"Let's see. I love pumpkin pie at Thanksgiving, foggy mornings, and Star Wars movies."

Sonora laughed—his intended response—and he joined her. They'd been playing this game for the last several days. Listing things they liked and other facts about themselves. He stored away every one of her answers like treasures. The more he knew, the more he wanted to know.

And while Graham realized that all of this was new to them both, he sensed something deeper there. Something that defied conventional logic that said there was no way he could know if she was right for him after a few weeks of interaction. It pushed past their age gap and past the things they hadn't yet shared the heart of it all.

"What are you thinking?" Sonora asked.

Swaying back and forth, he looked down at her and decided to be blunt. "I was thinking that I'm falling for you, Sonora Jackson."

She blinked but didn't look away.

"I know it's only been a short time, and I know that there is still so much to learn about one another, but I know the flecks of dark gray in your eyes, the way you care about others and want to help them, and how you like your hot cocoa." He bent down and brushed a kiss to the soft spot behind her ear. "And while I will never rush you or push you to do something you're not ready for, I want you to know that I'm in this—with you—for as long as you'll have me."

He caught her soft gasp and wondered if he'd gone too far, but when he pulled back to look at her again, she was smiling.

"Am I dreaming?"

He threw his head back and laughed. "If you are, then I am too. Can we agree to never wake up?"

"Yes."

Her smile shot straight to his heart. *Marry me, Sonora.*

He held the words in, knowing it wasn't the right time. But they were there, ready for when she was. When *they* were.

THIRTY-SEVEN

SONORA REACHED up and cupped Graham's cheek, the scratch of his light beard now familiar against her own skin. This was bliss. Dancing with the man she, too, was falling for under twinkling white lights on Christmas Eve.

"You're turn," he said. "What are you thinking about?"

"I can't remember a better Christmas." The honest answer was easy to admit to Graham.

She trusted him, even in the short span of time they'd known one another. She'd been hesitant about him at first, but he'd never done anything to indicate he was anything but the man she saw standing in front of her now. The man with integrity, heart, and a bit of a nerdy side.

"Me too," he agreed.

He spun her out and back as the music shifted. She came back into his arms and felt the rightness of it. Of him. They moved in sync as if they'd danced together for years though it had only been days, really. He anticipated her needs, listened to her every thought, and best of all, made her laugh.

Was this what love felt like?

He spun her again, and this time when she came back, she

nestled closer to him, relishing the strength of his arms and the sureness of his steps. He led her gently but confidently.

"I have a question for you, Sonora," he asked.

His lips whispered against her ear, sending chills down her spine. They stopped where his hand lightly rested against the bare part of her back.

"Ask away." She smiled up at him.

"What are you doing New Year's Eve?"

She laughed. "Do you know that's an Ella Fitzgerald song?"

"Nope." He chuckled. "But the question stands."

"I was kind of thinking of going to bed early." He frowned, which made her laugh again. "I have no plans, Mr. Hastings."

"And what about Valentine's Day?"

Sonora felt a light blush creep across her cheeks at Graham's gaze. "None then either."

"And Easter? And—"

"No plans."

The intensity in his eyes deepened as he leaned closer. "Would you consider spending them with me?"

A flutter of nerves skittered through her. Was she being hasty? Their age gap didn't seem to bother him, but was agreeing to indefinite plans with Graham smart? Was there something—anything—about him that she wasn't seeing clearly?

Her eyes traced the lines of his brow down to his slightly crooked nose then to the depths of his eyes, their golden hue deepened in the dim light. Her gaze stuttered on his lips, parted in anticipation of what she would say. Then back to his eyes.

She knew the answer. Even if she tried to talk herself out of it, her heart would rebel. He was what she wanted in a man. Kind, caring, wise, and willing to learn. Their ages didn't matter because her heart knew the truth.

"Yes." She slipped her fingers under the lapel of his tux and gently tugged him closer. "Yes to everything with you, Graham Hastings."

When their lips met, it was pure joy. Hope and expectation

combined with the sweetness of their passion and acted like a stamp on Sonora's heart. A reminder of this moment. How Graham's arms wrapped around her, pulling her close. The safety she felt there.

The spice of his cologne and the warmth of the room sent her head spinning as he snaked his hand into the loose waves of her hair. His thumb gently caressing her jaw. The kiss was one of passion and promise, and she fell headlong into it despite the fact they still swayed in the middle of the dance floor.

She was breathless when he pulled back, the depth of her emotions flushing her face with heat. He laughed, seeing her embarrassment, and pulled her against him, tucking her head under his chin.

"Sorry." His voice was husky. "Got a little carried away there."

A giggle escaped, and she felt it reciprocated by the rumble in his chest. "I'm not going to complain."

The music shifted again, and Sonora eased back so she could see Graham. He smiled down at her, the picture of confidence.

"I don't think I'll ever get tired of kissing you."

"Me either." Sonora slipped her hand into his. "Let's go get some cake."

"Shouldn't we wait for the dinner?"

Her eyes narrowed. "Why, when there's dessert?"

"I like the way you think," he said with a laugh.

"Then lead the way."

"Gladly." He paused for a moment to brush his lips to hers, pulling her close. "But nothing will ever be as sweet to me as your lips."

She felt it again in that moment, deep inside. The sense that their future was entwined. That no matter how they'd met and the lies that she'd put between them, it was always supposed to end like this. With her in his arms at Christmastime.

EPILOGUE

SIX MONTHS *later*

Blythe Lockwood stared at her computer, eyes crossing. Pushing back from the desk, she reached for her phone just as it pinged.

SONORA: Oh my gosh. I can't believe I'm here!

The text was followed by a photo of Sonora and Graham against a desert backdrop with sparse trees and grass-roofed huts in the distance.

Tears flooded Blythe's eyes at the pure joy on her friend's face.

BLYTHE: I'm so happy for you! Tell Prince Charming he'd better keep an eye on you.

SONORA: LOL. He hasn't let me out of his sight yet—I think we're safe on that front.

Blythe took a deep breath, admiring the photo again and the way Graham's eyes were focused on Sonora. It was clear to see the love written in his expression.

BLYTHE: Good. Go change the world, friend. I love you!

Blythe put her phone back down, the emptiness demanding her attention more forcefully than she'd expected. She was beyond happy for Sonora. She'd found a guy who truly loved her, not someone like Jonah who wanted to control her, and they were close to a proposal. Sonora hadn't said it, but Graham's look said it all.

But if she was truly happy for Sonora, what was she feeling?

Sitting with the emotion, the ugly truth reared its head. Blythe was jealous.

"Ugh." She dropped her head into her hands. "Stop it. Just—"

"Boss?"

Blythe jerked upright to see seventeen-year-old Maddox standing in the doorway with a tablet in one hand and a narrow-eyed expression. "You okay?"

"Yes. Of course I am."

"You were talking to yourself."

"It was a pep talk. We all need those sometimes."

Maddox didn't look convinced. "Right."

"What do you need?" Blythe asked, shifting into boss-mode.

"I wanted you to check that I got all the details right for this advertisement." Maddox approached her desk, handing over the tablet.

An image of the lodge covered in snow sat next to a photo of the nearby ski park, Cypress Mountain. Below, bold text highlighted the partnership with the resort and the Lockwood Lodge. It was Blythe's next great idea—or so she hoped.

"It looks good. Really good, Maddox."

"Yeah?" The teen grinned.

"Yeah. I'm continually impressed by your skills."

"Thanks." Maddox's cheeks reddened. "So, go to print?"

"Have LaToya look over it too, just in case. Then yes, print it."

"You got it, boss. Thanks."

She watched the teen slip out of her office. He was well on his way to becoming a great graphic designer, and she knew she'd miss him when he left for college.

Sighing, she leaned back in her chair again, spinning to face the window she'd had installed a month earlier. Gone was the blank wall of her office, and in its place, tall evergreens and spindly maples filled the view in all of their early summer glory.

And just in time, too. They'd be hosting wealthy guests in just a week for a Libertas summer experience. She liked the roving nature of the retreat, but it also meant changing up plans each year.

Blythe refocused on the digital brochure. She hoped adding the ski park package to their wintertime offerings would draw in new guests. Her grandfather had thought it was a great idea, but Blythe didn't know.

Why was she always plagued by self-doubt when it came to her own ideas?

Maybe because you have no idea what you're doing?

Blythe pushed away the negative self-talk. She'd had their accountant run the numbers three times, she'd asked several business friends in her mastermind group, and she'd checked with Grandfather. Shouldn't that be all the confidence-boosting she needed?

And yet, she still hesitated when it came to moving forward with her own plans.

The Lockwoods were a tough family to live up to. Her phone pinged again.

> SONORA: Love you too!

Blythe smiled at the text on the international app. The earlier jealousy diminished as Blythe thought about all she had to do. Prep for the Libertas Retreat, send out marketing materials to the PR firm her grandfather had suggested, and oversee the renovations to the north wing and second dining room.

Not to mention her day-to-day schedule, clearing up guest issues, and managing her teams of workers. It was coming up on their busiest time of year, and Blythe had no free mental space to spare.

And what? She wanted a boyfriend? How would that work?

Blythe stood, rolling her shoulders back and thrusting her chin out. She was Blythe Lockwood, manager of the Lockwood Lodge, and she didn't need a man in her life. No matter how much she might want one.

A REQUEST

If you enjoyed this book, I'd love it if you'd consider sharing a review on Amazon, Goodreads, or anywhere else you review. As an indie author, reviews help me *so* much, and they really do act as some of the best support a reader can give.

Thank you!

- Emilie (Aka Bell)

Dear reader,

Thank you for picking up another Christmas book from me. I've got to be honest…this one was a wild card.

When I first had the idea for the Lockwood Lodge Series following the completion of my Winter, Montana Christmas Series, I envisioned a different main character for this first book. And a different plot. What happened is what you find in these pages—a lot of sweet Christmas romance *and* some light suspense.

I wasn't sure how it was going to play out, but Sonora's background was so integral to the story I couldn't take it out. *Safe Haven* is a favorite movie of mine (yes, movie—not the book) but I also wanted to keep the romantic feelings without too much suspense. I hope I walked that balance beam well.

Another thing that surprised me about Sonoras story was her relationship with Jonah. (Side note here? His name was originally Nick and it hit me half-way through edits that I can't have my bad guy maned Nick in a *Christmas* book!)

Unfortunately, her story is not unlike many who face domestic abuse in all its forms. She felt the shame of that but, she was a victim as well as a survivor. Writing her happy ending was a blessing, but it doesn't take away from the fact that there are those out there who still struggle in abusive relationships.

My hope and prayer is that this story was enjoyable but also a good reminder that, especially at Christmastime, we can be on the look out to support and encourage those around us.

If you or someone you know is facing domestic violence don't wait for things to get better. Call 1-800-799-7233.

ACKNOWLEDGMENTS

A story is never completed alone. It's the culmination of hours of work for the writer, yes, but there are so many other aspects that go into crafting a novel.

First and foremost, I thank my Savior, Jesus, for the inspiration to write books of all kinds. If you know me at all you know I am multi-passionate and I attribute that to the person He has made me. I craft these stories to encourage and entertain others, but ultimately they are for Him.

Thanks to my husband, Alex. He puts up with many nights of me saying "I don't know what's for dinner" and helps out so much while I'm on deadlines!

Thanks to my awesome writers huddle: Steff, Natalie, and Christen. You gal's keep me grounded and on task!

Thanks to my amazing editor Meghan and proofreader, Connie.

Speaking of Connie, thanks to her and my dad, Mike. It's our time spent watching Hallmark movies that have always inspired these Christmas stories.

Thank you to my amazing readers! Somehow you show up for ALL that I write and don't seem to mind if it's in a small mountain town or the far reaches of space. You make this sometimes lonely pursuit totally worth it!

And finally, as the dedication says, thanks to all the nerds out there (myself included). When I realized that Graham likes space operas and dressing up for Comic-Con it made me love him even more.

AVAILABLE NOW

Come visit Winter, Montana where the Christmas lights are always on and the snow falls most frequently when loved ones share a kiss.

SCAN HERE

COMPLETE WINTER MONTANA SERIES

BOOK 1

BOOK 2

BOOK 3

BOOK 4

BOOK 5

LAST CHANCE FIRE & RESCUE

Expired Promise
Lisa Phillips presents Emilie Haney

EMT Andi Crawford has reached probationary status as a firefighter with the Eastside Firehouse, but the daily challenges of a female firefighter fade to the background when her family becomes the target of a dangerous drug cartel.

Andi will stop at nothing to protect her family. Even if that means accepting help she doesn't think she needs.

ATF Agent Jude Brooks is back in Last Chance County tasked with uncovering information on the family that took him in during his summers as a teen. As he wades through a web of leads, his feelings for Andi resurface.

He's determined to uncover the truth—for her and himself. If the secrets of the past don't tear them apart.

SCAN HERE

JOIN MY NEWSLETTER

Sing up to receive information about writing news, new releases, sales, and book-related information from me!

This newsletter covers several of the genres I write under the name Emilie Haney including (but not limited to): Romantic Suspense, Mystery, Cozy Mystery, and also Sweet Romance (under my pen name Bell Renshaw).

*No spam - ever!

SCAN HERE

Or visit my website:

EMILIEHANEY.COM

Bell Renshaw is a pen name for Emilie Haney

Emilie grew up in the Pacific Northwest and has a love for the outdoors that matches her love for the written word. She turned her passion for stories toward writing at an early age, finding entertainment and adventure in made-up worlds fed by the books her parents read to her as a child. Now, she's still getting lost in those worlds but they are of her own making.

She believes that—no matter what—love fights for what's right.

Find Bell Renshaw on Goodreads
Find Emilie Haney on Goodreads (*coming 2023*)
www.emiliehaney.com
emiliehaneyauthor@gmail.com

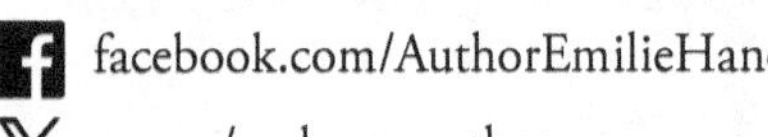

facebook.com/AuthorEmilieHaney

x.com/emhaneyauthor

instagram.com/emiliehaney_author

GENRE GUIDE

Emilie is multi-passionate when it comes to genre writing. Why stick to one when you could write several?

Here is a guide to what you can expect from each name she uses:

Emilie Haney
romantic suspense, mystery, cozy mystery

Bell Renshaw
sweet romance and rom-com

E. A. Hendryx
Science Fiction & Fantasy

www.ingramcontent.com/pod-product-compliance
Lightning Source LLC
Chambersburg PA
CBHW032247310726